WINNER OF THE COSTA FIRST NOVEL AWARD 2007

GALAXY BRITISH BOOK AWARD NEWCOMER OF THE YEAR 2008

WINNER OF THE JELF GROUP FIRST NOVEL AWARD 2007

SHORTLISTED FOR GUARDIAN FIRST NOVEL PRIZE 2007

SHORTLISTED FOR THE SOUTH BANK SHOW LITERATURE AWARD 2007

SHORTLISTED FOR THE COMMONWEALTH WRITERS' PRIZE 2007

LONGLISTED FOR THE MAN BOOKER PRIZE 2007

LONGLISTED FOR THE ORANGE BROADBAND PRIZE 2007

BBC RADIO FIVE LIVE BOOK OF THE MONTH MARCH 2007

'Hugely compelling and inventive, it pulls the rug from under your feet from the very first page – O'Flynn reveals her clues tantalisingly in this poignant story of love and loss'

Costa Prize Judges

'An off-beat, quirky mystery which punches way above its weight. The icing on the cake is the twist which I really didn't see coming'

Marian Keyes

'It's quite extraordinary. There's an amazing insight into the mind of a young girl, a very funny account of working in a high-street record store, an entirely sympathetic hero in the form of a security guard, a cracking mystery, a brilliant sense of place in the form of a modern shopping centre, and a ghost story to boot. I adored every page of it and recommend it to everyone'

Jenny Colgan

'This smartly written debut combines an unsettling personal story with a long, hard look at modern urban life. Inventive and humorous, O'Flynn saves her best lines for the more monstrous members of the retail trade' *Independent*

'*What Was Lost* starts off as a straightforward and extremely likeable account of a little girl who sets up a detective agency to honour her dead father. And then the book abruptly cuts from 1984 to 2003. Green Oaks, pallid as it was 20 years previously, is still there. Kate is not. The transition is remarkable. O'Flynn never abandons her wry sense of humour, but as she begins to tease out the connections between the two halves of her brilliantly conceived plot, the sense that something's missing grows stronger and stronger. The masterstroke of that unexpected shift is to make it feel as if the novel itself mourns the absence of its heroine; the irony, of course, is that her presence is felt on every line' *Spectator*

'O'Flynn's poignant first novel explores bereavement and loneliness, what it is to be invisible and what it takes to be found. Her prose is taut, and the story intricately plotted and compelling' *Telegraph*

'An exceptional, polyphonic novel of urban disaffection, written with humour and pathos. Kate's deceptively jaunty diary reveals a consumer-driven society choking on its own loneliness; a ghost story; and an examination of unspeakable loss' *Guardian*

'It's wonderful: an uncanny tale that begins in 1984 with ten-year-old Kate, who enjoys pretending to be a private detective until she goes missing. A beguiling novel about disconnection, loss and the anonymity of modern Britain' *Metro*

‘A delight to read – poignant, suspenseful, funny and smart. *What Was Lost* is a moving novel, bespeaking not only the energy and inventiveness of its author but also the power of good old realism’
Jane Smiley, *Los Angeles Times*

‘O’Flynn is just the colleague you’d want to be stuck with in a dead-end job’ *Literary Review*

‘Such is the sheer quality of writing, characterisation and skilful construction that it is hard to believe this is a first novel. O’Flynn deftly combines humour, love, loss and grief. Contemporary literary prose at its finest’ *Publishing News*

‘A mystery set among the shop workers of a huge shopping centre, *What Was Lost* is very spooky. A girl disappears but the dominating theme is the vast centre, which has an almost malignant influence in a very special novel indeed’ *Bookseller*

‘A comedy about a pint-sized girl detective and a group of disaffected record shop employees . . . O’Flynn’s spooky debut has a unique charm’ Matt Thorne

‘Tough and tender, witty and wise, this brilliant, compelling mystery rips the wrapping off 21st-century Britain, to expose haunting crimes in hidden lives’ Helen Cross

‘I love this book. It’s sad but funny with lots of wonderful modern themes about our way of living. At the heart of the success of this book is the incredible way that Catherine O’Flynn writes about this ten-year-old girl whom I absolutely loved as a character. It’s an absolute revelation’ Shami Chakrabarti

What Was Lost

Catherine O'Flynn

Tindal Street Press

First published in 2007 by Tindal Street Press Ltd
This edition published 2012 by Tindal Street Press Ltd
217 The Custard Factory, Gibb Street, Birmingham, B9 4AA
www.tindalstreet.co.uk

A CIP catalogue reference for this book is available from the British Library

ISBN: 978 1 906994 25 9

Typeset by Country Setting, Kingsdown, Kent

Printed and bound in Great Britain by
CPI Group (UK) Ltd, Croydon, CR0 4YY

Written for Peter,
and dedicated to the memory
of Donal of Hillstreet
and Ellen of Oylegate

Contents

1984

FALCON INVESTIGATIONS

1

Crime was out there. Undetected, unseen. She hoped she wouldn't be too late. The bus driver was keeping the bus at a steady 15 m.p.h., braking at every approaching green light until it turned red. She closed her eyes and continued the journey in her head as slowly as she could. She opened them, but still the bus lagged far behind her worst projection. Pedestrians overtook them, the driver whistled.

She looked at the other passengers and tried to deduce their activities for the day. Most were pensioners and she counted four instances of the same huge, blue checked shopping bag. She made a note of the occurrence in her pad; she knew better than to believe in coincidences.

She read the adverts on the bus. Most were adverts for adverts: 'If you're reading this, then so could your customers.' She wondered if any of the passengers ever took out advertising space on the bus, and what they would advertise if they did.

'Come and enjoy my big, blue, checked shopping bag, it is filled with catfood.'

'I will talk to anyone about anything. I also eat biscuits.'

'Mr and Mrs Roberts, officially recognized brewers of the world's strongest tea. "We squeeze the bag."'

'I smell strange, but not unpleasantly.'

Kate thought she would like to take out an advert for the agency. The image would be a silhouette of her and

Mickey within the lens of a magnifying glass. Below, it would say:

FALCON INVESTIGATIONS
Clues found. Suspects trailed.
Crimes detected.
Visit our office equipped with
the latest surveillance equipment.

She made another note in her pad of the phone number on the advert, to be rung at some later date when the office was fully operational.

Eventually the bus reached the landscaped lawns and forlorn, fluttering flags of the light industrial estates that surrounded the newly opened Green Oaks Shopping Centre. She paid particular attention to unit 15 on the Langsdale Estate, where she had once witnessed what seemed to be an argument between two men. One man had a large moustache, the other wore sunglasses and no jacket on what had been a cold day – she'd thought they both looked of criminal character. After some deliberation and subsequent sightings of a large white van outside the unit, she had come to the conclusion that the two men were trafficking diamonds. Today all was quiet at the unit.

She opened her pad at a page with 'Unit 15 Surveillance' written at the top. Next to that day's date she wrote in the slightly jerky bus writing that dominated the page: 'No sighting. Collecting another shipment from Holland?'

Fifteen minutes later Kate was walking through the processed air of the Market Place of Green Oaks. Market Place wasn't a market place. It was the subterranean part of the shopping centre, next to the bus terminals, reserved for the non-prestige, low-end stores: fancy goods stores, cheap chemists, fake perfume sellers, stinking butchers, flammable-clothes vendors. Their smells mingled with the smell of burnt dust from the over-door heaters and made her feel sick. This was as far as most of Kate's fellow passengers ventured into the centre. It was the closest approximation of the tatty old High Street, which had suffered a rapid decline since the centre had opened. Now when the bus drove up the High Street no one liked to look at the reproachful boarded up doorways filled with fast-food debris and leaves.

She realized that it was Wednesday and that she'd forgotten to buy that week's copy of the *Beano* from her usual newsagent. She had no choice but to go to the dingy kiosk in the centre to get it. Afterwards she stood and looked again at the *True Detective* magazines on the shelf. The woman on the front didn't look like a detective. She was wearing a trilby and raincoat . . . but nothing else. She looked like someone from a *Two Ronnies* sketch. Kate didn't like it.

She rode the escalator up to the ground floor, where the proper shops, the fountains and plastic palms began. It was the school holidays, but too early to be busy. None of her classmates was allowed to go to the centre without their parents. Sometimes she'd bump into a family group with one of her peers in tow and would exchange awkward greetings. She had picked up a sense that adults tended to be uncomfortable with her solo trips out and about, so now whenever questioned by shop assistant, security guard or parent she would always imply that an unspecified adult relative was just off in another store. Largely, though, no one questioned her, in fact no one ever really seemed to see her at all. Sometimes Kate thought she was invisible.

It was 9.30 a.m. She retrieved her laboriously type-written agenda from her back pocket:

09.30–10.45	Tandy: research walkie talkies and microphones
10.45–12.00	general centre surveillance
12.00–12.45	lunch at Vanezi's
12.45–13.30	Midland Educational: look at ink pads for fingerprinting
13.30–15.30	surveillance by banks
15.30	bus home

Kate hurried on to Tandy.

She was flustered to arrive at Vanezi's restaurant a good twenty minutes past noon. This was not the way a professional operated. This was sloppy. She waited by the door to be seated, though she could see her table was still free. The same lady as usual took her to the same table as usual and Kate slid into the orange plastic booth which offered a view out over the main atrium of the centre.

'Do you need to see the menu today?' asked the waitress.

'No thanks. Can I have the Children's Special please with a banana float? And can I not have any cucumber on the beefburger, please?'

'It's not cucumber, it's gherkin, love.'

Kate made a note of this in her pad: 'Gherkins/cucumbers – not same thing: research difference.' She'd hate to blow her cover on a Stateside mission with a stupid error like that.

Kate looked at the big plastic tomato-shaped tomato-sauce dispenser on her table. They were one of her favourite things – they made total sense.

At school last term, Paul Roberts had read out his essay, 'The best birthday ever', which culminated in his grandparents and parents taking him out to Vanezi's for dinner. He spoke of eating spaghetti with meatballs, which for some reason he and everyone else in the class had found funny. He was still excited as he rushed through his story of drinking ice-cream floats and ordering a Knickerbocker Glory. He said it was brilliant.

Kate couldn't understand why he didn't just take himself there on a Saturday lunchtime if he liked it so much. She could even take him the first time and tell him the best place to sit. She could show him the little panel on the wall that you could slide back to reveal all the dirty plates passing by on a conveyor belt. She could tell him how one day she hoped to place some kind of auto-shutter action camera on the belt, which could travel around the entire restaurant taking surveillance shots unseen, before returning to Kate. She could point out the washing-up man who she thought might be murderous, and perhaps Paul could help her stake him out. She could maybe invite him to join the agency (if Mickey approved). But she didn't say anything. She just wondered.

She glanced around to check that no one could see, then she reached into her bag and pulled out Mickey. She sat him next to her by the window, so that the waitress wouldn't notice, and where he had a good view of the people below. She was training Mickey up to be her partner in the agency. Generally Mickey just did surveillance work. He was small enough to be unobtrusive despite his rather outlandish get-up. Kate liked Mickey's outfit even though it meant he didn't blend in as well as he might. He wore a pin-striped gangster suit with spats. The spats slightly spoiled the Sam Spade effect, but Kate liked them anyway; in fact she wanted a pair herself.

Mickey had been made from a craft kit called 'Sew your own Charlie Chimp the Gangster' given to Kate by an auntie. Charlie had languished along with all of Kate's other soft toys throughout most of her childhood, but when she'd started up the detective agency last year she thought he looked the part. Charlie Chimp was no good though.

Instead he became Mickey the Monkey. Kate would run through their agenda with him each morning and he always travelled with her in the canvas army surplus bag.

The waitress brought the order. Kate ate the burger and perused the first *Beano* of the new year, while Mickey kept a steady eye on some suspicious teenagers below.

2

Kate lived a bus journey away from Green Oaks. Her home was in the only Victorian block of houses left in the area, a red-brick three-storey outcrop which looked uncomfortable amidst the grey and white council-built cuboids. Kate's house was sandwiched between a newsagent's shop on one side, and a butcher and greengrocer on the other. Her house had clearly also been a shop once, but now a net curtain hung across the front window and what had been the shop was a sitting room where Kate's grandmother spent her long afternoons watching quiz shows.

The house was the only one in the block not to function as a business (aside from Kate's putative agency operation), and it was also the only one used as a home. None of her shopkeeper neighbours lived above their shops; at around six o'clock each evening they would shut up and depart for their semis in the suburbs, leaving silence and emptiness on all sides of Kate's room.

Kate knew and liked the shopkeepers well. The greengrocer's was run by Eric and his wife Mavis. They had no children, but they were always kind to Kate and bought her a surprisingly well-judged Christmas present each year. Last year it had been a Spirograph, which Kate had used to make a professional-looking logo on her business cards. Now her time was taken up with the agency and constant surveillance activity, Kate had less time to visit the couple, but still once a week she would pop in for a cup of tea and, swinging her legs from the stool behind the counter, she would listen to Radio 2 and watch the customers buy vast quantities of potatoes.

Next to Eric and Mavis was Mr Watkin the butcher. Mr Watkin was an old man, Kate estimated probably seventy-eight. He was a nice man with a nice wife, but very few people bought their meat from him any more. Kate thought this possibly had something to do with the way Mr Watkin stood in his shop window swatting flies against the sides of meat with a large palette knife. It was also perhaps a self-perpetuating situation, in that the fewer customers Mr Watkin had, the less meat he stocked, and the less meat he had, the less he looked like a butcher, and the more he looked like a crazy old man who collected and displayed bits of flesh in his front window. The previous week Kate had passed the window to see it contained only a single rabbit (and Kate was sure the only person alive who still ate rabbit was in fact Mr Watkin himself), some kidneys, a chicken, a side of pork and a string of sausages. This in itself was nothing too remarkable for Mr Watkin, but what caused Kate to stop and stare was an apparent new marketing initiative by the butcher. Evidently he had become a little embarrassed by the minimal nature of his window displays and so perhaps in order to make them seem less odd (and this is where Kate felt he'd really miscalculated), he had arranged the items in a jaunty tableau. Thus it appeared that the chicken was taking the rabbit for a walk by its lead of sausages, over a hillock of pork under a dark red kidney sun. Kate looked up from the grisly scene to see Mr Watkin nodding at her in amazement from inside the shop, thumbs aloft, as if taken aback by his own flair.

On the other side of Kate's house was Mr Palmer the newsagent. Mr Palmer worked alongside his son Adrian, who was the closest Kate had to a best friend, and was also the first and so far only client of Falcon Investigations.

Adrian was twenty-two and had been to university. Mr Palmer had wanted Adrian to get a 'proper career' after graduation, but Adrian had no such ambitions, and was happy to spend his days reading behind the counter and helping to run the small business. The Palmer family lived in a modern semi on the outskirts of town, but the mother and sister rarely visited the shop – sweet selling was left to the men of the family. Adrian treated Kate like an adult, but then Adrian treated everyone the same. He wasn't capable of putting on a different face for different customers as his father did. Mr Palmer could switch from an avuncular 'Now then, young man', to an utterly sincere 'Such a shocking headline, isn't it, Mrs Stevens?' in seconds.

But, whatever Adrian's enthusiasms were, he tended to assume they were shared by all, or at least would be if he spread the word. He spent his afternoons buried in the *NME* or reading books about musicians. He would earnestly recommend albums to his customers, seemingly blind to the improbability of Mrs Docherty suddenly switching from Foster and Allen to the MC5, or Debbie Casey and her giggling teenage pals ever finding much of significance in Leonard Cohen. As soon as Mr Palmer left him alone in the shop, Jimmy Young's radio show would be switched off and Adrian would slip a tape into the tinny radio cassette player. He thought that the reason no one ever asked him what was playing was because they were a little shy, so he would always put a scrawled sign on the counter: 'Now Playing: Captain Beefheart, *Lick My Decals Off, Baby*. For more information just ask a member of staff'.

With Kate, though, Adrian liked to talk about crime detection, about classic detective movies, about which customers might be killers, about where they might have hidden their victims' bodies. Adrian would always come up with the most inventive body dumps. Sometimes Kate would go with Adrian to the wholesalers, advising him on what sweets to buy, and they would look at the burly warehousemen and assess which of them had criminal records.

Adrian knew about Falcon Investigations, though not about Mickey. Mickey was top secret. Mr Palmer had been getting increasingly irate about schoolkid sweet pilfering and so Adrian contracted Falcon Investigations to carry out a security assessment of the store. Kate told him that her rate was £1 a day plus expenses. She said she expected the assessment to take half a day at the most and no expenses would be incurred as she lived next door, and so she prepared an invoice for 50p. Kate was indescribably elated at this 'proper' commission. She even went out and bought a real invoice pad with duplicate sheets, which at 75p put the P&L in deficit, but she was building for the future. Kate asked Adrian to act as he normally would do when working in the shop and she played the part of a shoplifter. She said this was essential for her to pinpoint weak spots. After twenty minutes Kate left the shop and returned to the office to write up the report. She presented it to Adrian a couple of hours later, along with 37p worth of sweets she had managed to lift. The report was in two parts, the first detailing her time in the shop, the second making recommendations to 'stamp out crime'. These involved a rearrangement of some of the loose pocket-money sweets, a complete overhaul of the crisp display rack and the positioning of two mirrors at strategic points.

Adrian treated the report with the seriousness in which it had been compiled and carried out the recommendations to the letter. Mr Palmer was delighted with the results and pilfering was brought to a virtual standstill. Kate asked Mr Palmer if he would write down any positive comments he had about the service, as she had seen other businesses use such personal testimonials on promotional material.

She imagined her advert on the bus garlanded with sincere plaudits:

'We received a rapid, professional service at very reasonable rates.'

'Our agent was confidential, tactful and most of all EFFECTIVE.'

'Crime rates have plummeted since we called in Falcon Investigations.'

She was then slightly disappointed to receive instead from Mr Palmer: 'Good girl, Kate! You're a little treasure!!'

3

Each time she visited Green Oaks, Kate always paid a visit to Midland Educational, the large stationery store. Today's ostensible reason had been to examine their range of ink pads, but Kate always found some excuse to spend time in the store. Hours flew by.

Although Sam Spade is not seen at any point during *The Maltese Falcon* shopping for stationery, Kate knew how important premium office supplies were to an effective investigator. In fact stationery was something of a growing problem for Kate. At the start of last term, she had been taken for the first time into the stationery cupboard at school. Mrs Finnegan told Kate that she would be Stationery Monitor and gave her a thorough run-through of her forthcoming duties and responsibilities. She was puzzled as to why the always attentive Kate seemed lost in a world of her own.

Mrs Finnegan: It is vital that for every new exercise book given out you must collect the signed corner snipping from the old, filled exercise book. These must be collected in this Tupperware container and at the end of the week the number in the container must correspond exactly with the decrease in the number of exercise books you record in the Audit Register. Does that all make sense, Kate?

Kate: . . .

Mrs Finnegan: Kate?

Kate had not been prepared for the level of riches in the

stationery cupboard. First, it was not a cupboard, it was a room. Secondly, it was evident that the full range of stationery she and her classmates had ever used were but tiny and very dull drops in the vast ocean of the cupboard. The room contained luxury items like multi-coloured Biros, metal pencil sharpeners, entire packets of felt-tips alongside serious, high-end items like concertina files and jumbo staplers. Kate didn't hear a word Mrs Finnegan said because she was in a state of actual, physical shock.

Since that afternoon the cupboard had played on her mind. She knew it was important for an investigator to get inside the criminal mind, but she suspected the motives of her brain's endless inventiveness in how to run rings around the audit register. She feared she was being pulled towards corruption.

Today in Midland Educational she had spent thirty minutes looking at ink stamps, trying to think of a reason for needing one but failing. Now Kate was doing her usual stint outside the banks and building societies. She had been watching them for over an hour. Two banks and three building societies were all situated next to each other on level 2 of the centre next to the children's play area. Between them was an oasis of imitation plant life surrounded by orange plastic seats. Kate sat with Mickey poking discreetly out of the bag by her side.

She had always thought if any significant crime was going to happen at the centre it would have to be here. She was sure of it. The security guards were all too busy watching shoplifters and truants, but Kate had her eye on the big picture and one day the hours she put in would pay off. Sometimes she allowed herself to think about the kind of civic reception she'd get when she foiled her first major robbery. In the *Beano*, good deeds were rewarded with a 'slap-up meal' invariably consisting of a mountain of mashed potato with sausages poking out. Kate hoped for something more like a medal or badge and maybe an ongoing role working alongside adult detectives.

Radio Green Oaks chattered in the background as she watched the blank faces of the people gliding in and out of the banks. She watched people draw hundreds of pounds out, as if in a daze. A young couple each with five or six carrier bags from the fashion stores floated over, withdrew £100 each and then drifted back towards the shops. Their glassiness was part of a wider unreal feeling in the centre. No one appeared to have a purpose; they would drift into Kate's path and then block her way, seeming to just walk on the spot. Sometimes it scared her. She thought she might be the only living thing in Green Oaks. Other times she thought that perhaps she was a ghost haunting the lanes and escalators.

She knew that one day she would see someone by the banks with a different look on their face. Anxiety, or cunning, or hate, or desire, and she would know that they were a suspect. So she scanned the faces for any flicker of deviance. Her eyes moved over the play area where there were some children her own age looking unimpressed with the facilities. They were too old for the jungle fantasy and the ball pool, but unlike Kate they didn't seem to realize that the whole centre was an enormous playground. She felt the dull ache of loneliness in her stomach, but her brain didn't register it. It was old news.

Kate's favourite book, *How to be a Detective* (part of the Junior Factfinder series), was quite explicit about the sore feet and boredom necessary to crack crime. You had to put the hours in all day, every day:

The best detectives are always prepared – day or night. They can be called upon at any time to investigate crimes or follow suspects. Crooks are cunning and love the cover of darkness.

It was classified top-secret information, but Kate had spent a night at Green Oaks. She'd typed a note home about a fabricated school trip away and had set off with Mickey, a flask and her notebook. She got to the centre just before it closed and hid in the little plastic house in the middle of the children's play area. She waited there, until the shop-workers went home and the muzak was turned off. She'd tried to stay awake all night, watching the banks from inside the house, getting out every now and then to take a closer look and stretch her legs. She must have fallen asleep just before dawn; when she woke up the banks were open and the first customers were already there. Luckily Mickey, professional as ever, had remained alert, so nothing had been missed. She was disappointed with her lack of stamina though. She was determined to try again and next time to stay awake all night.

The man sitting two seats away got up and walked away and Kate realized with annoyance that he had been sitting there for a long time, but that she hadn't seen his face. Maybe he was casing Lloyds, maybe his face showed a concentrated expression. She got up to follow him, but changed her mind when she realized she should be getting home. She put an entry for her surveillance shift into her notebook, stuffed Mickey's head back into her bag and headed for the bus.

4

TOP SECRET. DETECTIVE NOTEBOOK.
PROPERTY OF AGENT KATE MEANEY.

Thursday 19th April
Man with the suntan and checked sports jacket in Vanezi's again. He has new steel-rimmed dark glasses. Think he is American, looks like bad men in *Columbo*. Suspect he is a hired assassin staking out a subject. Beginning to think this could be the waitress with no neck. He stared at her a lot. Have yet to discover motive for her murder, but will attempt to engage her in casual conversation tomorrow and if necessary I will warn her, but need more evidence on 'Mr Tan' first.

When leaving he dropped a lighter as he passed my table, think it was an attempt to view my notes. I quickly slid the book under my menu and he disguised his frustration. He is perhaps beginning to realize I am a worthy opponent.

Friday 20th April
No Mr Tan today, but instead a woman with a suspiciously bad wig. Are they connected??? She was extremely collected, and showed no signs of anxiety as she ate her Black Forest Gateau.

No-neck waitress nowhere to be seen – asked the waitress who served me about her and was told it was her 'day off'. Interesting.

Saturday 21st April
Back to Vanezi's today. Mr Tan as ever back in his corner seat. Mrs Wig also present but now have no suspicions of any connection with Tan. Saw her take many pills from various bottles – could be wig is for medical rather than criminal reasons.

Woman in blue raincoat spotted once more on bench outside Mothercare. Today she had a pushchair, but still no child.

Tuesday 24th April
Nothing to report today. Man seen eating orange peel from brown paper bag. Followed him for 40 minutes but no further deviance observed.

Spent two hours outside banks – no one looked wrong.

Wednesday 25th April
Middle-aged man in tatty coat lost something in one of the bins. Saw him put his arm in and pull stuff out. Thought security guards were coming to help him, but instead they just led him off the premises. Noticed he had got confused and put an old hamburger that someone had thrown away in his pocket.

Decided against continuing search myself.

Thursday 26th April
Tall white male seen today hiding in tropical shrubbery area in central atrium. Appeared to be talking to a leaf. No criminal motive apparent and so Mickey and I moved away quickly.

Friday 27th April
Whilst observing the banks a lone male marched past me and burst into Barclays. Had no doubt that this was a raid. Followed him in with my camera, only to find him

shouting at the cashier about bank charges. He used a lot of bad language but was unarmed and seemed uninterested in holding up the bank. A useful drill, though – he caught us sleeping.

5

Mrs Finnegan had implemented a ground-breaking seating regime with Junior Three. It was not alphabetical as with Mr Gibbs; it was not the 'blue table, red table . . .' method favoured by Mrs Cress; and it was not of course the dreamt of 'sit by your friend' favoured by every child (Mrs Cress had described this suggestion as 'outlandish').

It was instead a method which sought to attain complete equilibrium. The sum of intelligence, naughtiness, smelliness, noisiness in each two-desk-pairing would, as near as possible, be equal across the class. A noisy child would be teamed with a silent child, a naughty child teamed with a telltale.

Mrs Finnegan doubtless hoped to engender mistrust and despair: a class of informers and infighters. For the bulk of the class, however, her system had allowed them to sit next to their mates. The happy majority had no distinguishing features or traits and thus had to be paired with similarly unremarkable pupils, or perilous dominance and disequilibrium would occur.

For those few at the margins of the class, however, the system was punitive. Kate was deemed bright, well behaved, quiet and clean, and her reward for this was to be sat next to Teresa Stanton.

On their first day together Teresa had turned to Kate, said: 'Look!' and then promptly swallowed a 5p before opening her mouth and extending her tongue to prove it had gone. Kate yelped and buried her head in her workbook, but Teresa then proceeded to emit a series of disgusting inverted burp sounds, before a particularly violent one resulted in the 5p being expelled at force from some unspeakable wet cavity straight onto Kate's work.

Teresa had joined the class at the start of spring term, allegedly after being expelled from her last school, and her arrival had upset the accepted hierarchies and relationships that had been established in the class back in Infant One. Previously there had been an acknowledged naughtiest girl in the class and ahead of her was the naughtiest boy in the class. There was also a dirtiest boy and girl, and the oddest boy and girl . . . Whatever the distinction – naughtiest, loudest, most violent – the boys always fielded the most extreme candidate.

Now these former medal-winners looked on from the sidelines, confused and disorientated, as Teresa Stanton strolled past them to the finishing post in all events. Definitions had to be redrawn. A class of thirty children had grown up since the age of five believing Eamon Morgan's behaviour was the naughtiest behaviour possible. Once, when the universally feared Mrs Finnegan had left the room to get something from the stationery cupboard, Eamon had taken her place at the front of the classroom, performed a not terribly accurate but unbelievably daring impersonation of her, and then to the gasps and yelps of twenty-nine children, had written 'Bitch' in chalk on the blackboard. Kate had thought she might faint with fear when Mrs Finnegan had re-entered the room. No one in the class would forget that long afternoon of terror, cross-examination and threat, ending with Eamon finally owning up to save the rest of the class, and Mrs Finnegan's terrible smile when he did.

On Teresa's first day in class, evidently bored of Mrs Finnegan's lecture on the Principality of Wales, she yawned loudly and extensively and, apparently oblivious to all eyes in the class fixed on her, noisily threw her books in her desk, let the lid slam and simply walked out of the room. The class was thrown into chaos. Like a small tribal culture whose cosmology is suddenly torn apart by the arrival of a box of cornflakes, the class could not begin to assimilate this action into the world they knew. Walking out of school? They were taken to school in the morning, they were picked up in the evening, they sought permission to go to the toilet, they played in prescribed parts of the playground, they queued in a particular direction, they always walked on the left. The school was an intricate web of invisible force fields and boundaries; how could she cross a boundary that no one else had been able to see? In the days that followed, Teresa bombarded Junior Three with one unimaginable shock after another, perhaps the greatest of which was her utter obliviousness to Mrs Finnegan's rage.

On her first day in Mrs Finnegan's class, Kate had made the extremely difficult decision to wet herself rather than ask Mrs Finnegan if she could go to the toilet. Five years of hearing the screaming fury of Mrs Finnegan echo down corridors had helped Kate make this decision. And nothing she had seen of Mrs Finnegan's psychotic temper since joining her class had changed her mind. It was hard for the class to comprehend, but Mrs Finnegan really did seem to despise them all. Everything she said was soaked in a dark, acid sarcasm. Every day Mrs Finnegan said, 'Good morning, children,' and managed to imbue this simple greeting with so many layers of meaning, taunt and bitterness that it could make Kate feel sick.

Cruel humour was what the class expected and hoped for most days, because the alternative was when Mrs Finnegan lost her temper. The volume alone was enough to make their stomachs disappear, the viciousness was of a kind rarely heard outside the home, and often there was violence too. When his new skinhead haircut prevented Mrs Finnegan from pulling John Fitzpatrick's hair, she simply punched him instead.

But Teresa was unmoved by all this. This was not the bravado of Noel Brennan, who tried to smirk when Mrs Finnegan slapped him in the face; this was genuine indifference. It was as if Mrs Finnegan and indeed the rest of the class were simply not in Teresa's eyeline. As Mrs Finnegan screamed at Teresa and poked her to emphasize each syllable, Teresa stared blankly ahead as if watching an old cartoon with the sound down.

And then one day Mrs Finnegan finally found the volume control. Teresa was looking out of the window while Mrs Finnegan bellowed at her for having drawn monstrous faces on every page of her exercise book. At the end of this stream of invective, Mrs Finnegan, uncharacteristically seeming to concede defeat, said: 'Soon you will find yourself expelled again and next time, no school will take you, and then you will stay at home all day long and –'

Before she could finish, Teresa gave Mrs Finnegan her full attention for the first time. Her eyes filled with tears and then she sobbed uncontrollably for half an hour. Mrs Finnegan looked on in amazement, along with the rest of the class.

At breaktime everyone talked about Teresa's capitulation and the old deposed naughty boys tried to win back some credibility by claiming that being forced to stay at home would make them laugh, not cry. And it was true, this had seemed a most ineffectual threat by Mrs Finnegan, as ill-advised a strategy as the oft-attempted 'Eat your crusts or your hair won't go curly'.

From her seat next to Teresa, however, Kate understood. She saw bruises and burns on Teresa's legs and arms like she'd never seen before and she knew why Teresa wanted to be in school. Sometimes in the afternoons Teresa would stare out of the window and Kate would slip into a trance, staring at the edges of the bluey-black clouds that peeped out from beneath Teresa's sleeves.

6

After school one wet Thursday, Kate sat at the living-room table struggling to find something interesting to write about the Vikings. She looked in her textbook at sombre photographs of rusted metal fragments and broken pottery and her mind wandered. She remembered another occasion, working at the same spot, but on something that mattered. She had been making a neat grid with ruler and pencil and in the background Ella Fitzgerald had been singing about a lady who was a tramp. Her dad had sung along in the kitchen as he made fishfingers and chips for their tea.

'What's crab games, Dad?' Kate shouted through. She'd been wondering this for some time.

'What's what?'

'Crab games. She says "doesn't play crab games with barons and earls".' Kate had an image of men in monocles and robes shuffling sideways.

'It's not "crab games". It's "crap games",' he shouted.

Kate was a bit shocked.

'You know. It's some kind of dice game. They always talk about "shooting craps". It's what the hoods do when they aren't chasing classy broads, or dodging G-men. Ain't that right, sugar?' By now her father was talking in an appalling Brooklyn accent.

'Do all the people in New York talk like ducks, Dad?'

The response to this was a tea towel in her face, hurled through the serving hatch.

'Yes, that's right, talk like ducks and walk like crabs – it's quite a town. Anyway, are the results plotted yet?'

'Not yet, I'm still drawing the table.' Kate was using a ruler to make sure the grid lines were evenly spaced.

They had just finished their latest research project. This week's had been a wide-ranging *Which?*-style report on pear drops. Kate and her father shared a passion for them and had visited fifteen different sweet shops to compare size, sugar coating (or smooth), price per quarter pound, degree of acidity. Frank was a retired statistician and he and Kate spent much of their time together compiling neatly written reports and charts: the best tea shop in Warwickshire, the best salt and vinegar crisps, the grumpiest waitress ever. A definitive guide to the 10p mix-up was planned for the following month.

At sixty-one, Frank was far older than the parents of any of Kate's classmates, but it never bothered Kate. They had the best times together. Kate estimated that her dad was at least a hundred times more fun and interesting and clever than any other parents she saw. Some people in her class had just a mom and no dad, but Kate was the only child with a dad and no mom. Her mom had left when Kate was a toddler, and she had no memory of her at all. Kate sometimes wondered how they would ever have had room in their lives for another person; there was just no space for a mom to fill. Every weekend and school holiday were planned in advance. Trips to interesting cemeteries, gas works, factories, forgotten parts of the city. Frank peopling the local history with invented characters with silly names and ridiculous biographies. On weekday evenings Kate would sit on his lap, and the two of them watched TV together, always hoping for an old American black and white film on BBC2: gangsters, detectives, bad men, femme fatales, shadows and guns. They loved Humphrey DeForest Bogart, and they laughed every time they watched him make a sap out of Elisha Cook Jr or Peter Lorre. Frank would do terrible impressions and Kate would try and pepper her sentences with hard-boiled American vernacular.

'Hurry up, Dad. *The Rockford Files* is on in a minute.'

'Hurry up? Hurry up? Do you want uneven fishfingers? Do you think it's easy getting them exactly the same shade of fluorescent orange on each surface? Do you know how difficult it is to avoid "dark surface shading" as it's known in the best restaurants? Please do me the service of allowing me a free rein in the kitchen.'

'His answer phone is going – you're missing it.'

'That's the kind of sacrifice great artists have to make. I think Michelangelo missed some classic episodes of *Columbo* when he was finishing the Sistine Chapel. Picasso had never even heard of *Quincy*. Anyway, it's a repeat – they all are.'

Finally Frank passed two plates through the serving hatch, and they sat at the table watching as Jim Rockford discovered more than he bargained for on a fishing trip.

When the programme finished, Frank told Kate to go and look in the drawer in the front room. She came back with a small package wrapped in stripy wrapping paper.

'What is it?'

'It's a present for you.'

'Who from?'

'From me. Who do you think?'

'What for?'

'I told you I'd get you something when we finished the pear drop project.'

Kate was grinning. She had of course remembered this promise, but it didn't seem right to look as if she expected the present. She opened the package and inside was a book called *How to be a Detective*. Kate grinned again. She liked the look of the book.

'I thought we could solve some crimes together – I can be Sam Spade and you can be his assistant . . . whatshisname . . . Miles Archer.'

'He gets killed at the start of the film.'

'Well, yes, OK, but he didn't have this book – you'll be wised up. We can start off finding out who's been pinching our yoghurt that the milkman says he leaves every Friday.'

But Kate was flicking wide-eyed through the book, amazed at the possibilities opening up in front of her.

'Dad, we can do more than that. We can catch proper outlaws – bank robbers, kidnappers . . . Look, it shows you how to disguise yourself so you can get closer to the suspect . . . Look, a "tourist", brilliant – no one would suspect that you're actually taking photos of the criminals.'

'I think a tourist might be a bit conspicuous round here. This is Birmingham.'

'Or a window cleaner . . . Dad, this is a brilliant book. We're going to fight crime on the streets.'

But it hadn't worked out like that. A few months later Kate woke up one morning to find bright sunlight flooding her room. She had never been good at waking up and was amazed that for once she could surprise her dad by being sat up and casually reading when he brought her the morning cup of tea. She waited in bed listening for sounds of him shuffling in the kitchen while Radio 2 played easy country, but she could hear nothing. She re-read the pages on checking alibis in *How to be a Detective* and then finally, disgruntled that her surprise had been ruined, got up and went down to the kitchen. The fridge was open and inside she saw one of her dad's walking boots placed on top of the margarine. She called him, but there was no answer. Then in the kitchen sink she saw a pile of documents that had been half burnt and thrown into water. There was his bus pass, old notes, some junk mail and an article on statistical methods. As she walked back through the kitchen and into the lounge she noticed more and more things out of place, lots of little things wrong. This was a strange game.

She found her father lying on the bedroom floor. As she opened the door he seemed to be calling for her urgently but as she ran to him and knelt down by him, he didn't seem to see her and kept saying the same indistinguishable word over and over while his hand clutched again and again at some invisible airborne irritant. Kate was crying as she shook him, saying, 'Wake up, Dad, wake up,' but she knew he wasn't asleep. He didn't look like the dad she knew. His face seemed angry and he looked straight through her, even seeming to swat her away. She knew she should phone someone, but she couldn't imagine picking up the phone. She didn't know how she could talk about him as if he wasn't there.

Eventually the sirens came and her grandmother too. Her dad seemed particularly agitated by the ambulance driver's tie, trying to grab it while shouting a new word that sounded like 'Harry'. It was the last sound she heard him make. He died in hospital four hours later. Her grandmother told her he'd had a stroke. Kate couldn't understand. A stroke was a gentle, caring thing. Her dad always stroked her head when she couldn't sleep. She sat in the hospital corridor, staring at the door they'd taken him through, waiting to feel that soothing pressure again.

Since then life had been different. Kate's grandmother came to live with her. A widow whose only daughter had left Frank and Kate eight years earlier for her new life in Australia, Ivy had kept in contact with Frank over the years, sending cards, visiting on occasions, but she and Kate were virtual strangers.

Ivy presented herself to Kate and said: 'I won't have you going into care. I'm moving in so that won't happen. I wouldn't wish that on anyone. I'll cook for you and I'll live here with you. It makes no difference to me where I live any more. I'm sorry about your dad – I'm very sorry. It's not your fault he was so old, but I can't be your mom. I'm no good at that kind of thing. I tried it once and look where it got me. Your mother is a stupid woman. I'm sorry to say it, but it's true. She married a man twice her age and then ran off leaving you behind and now here I am picking up the pieces . . . again. I know you're a bright girl, and I know you're a good girl – so I'm sure we'll get along fine. The only thing you need to know about me is that I like watching quiz shows and I like going to bingo.'

Kate nodded and greeted this information with a great internal shrug.

She found the evenings long and empty, and the nights worse. She dreaded the weekends. She had learned not to think about Frank on that last night – his brain affected by the pressure of the blood, confused and alone, silently mixing up the house. She had learned that to think about that hurt so much it was dangerous.

She found the forgotten stuffed chimp in a cupboard and started Falcon Investigations. She occupied her mind with lists, surveillance, reports, projects. She worked hard at school, she kept quiet, she sat in the shop next door with Adrian, she moved from room to room in the big house.

7

Kate ran over the brow of the artificial hill. The sky was purple behind her and a gale blasted the ugly, spindly trees, bending and flicking their branches. The litter had escaped from the shrubs and now whipped in cyclones in the doorways of the maisonettes. A thunderstorm was coming and Kate could feel the air fizzing and sparking as she ran through it. The wind blew her faster as she leapt down the slope and ran and ran. She felt unbreakable as she ran past the shattered glass of the bus stop, over the landscaped undulations of the estate and through the deserted quadrangle. Washing snapped crazily on the lines in the quad and Kate ran through it blindly, breathing in the floral detergent as sheets wrapped around her face. She laughed and ran, past the school, past the shabby, kit-built Methodist church, leaping as she ran, feeling out of control, hoping that the wind would carry her off. As the first, fat blobs of rain splatted on the pavement she was running down her road. She wanted to get up to her window to watch the coming lightning sweep across the wires of the pylons.

Fifteen minutes later she sat glumly looking out at the soaked streets.

The sky had turned from violet to grey and the charged excitement of the coming storm deadened rapidly to the drab reality of a wet afternoon. She watched the drops of rain slide down the pane, blurring the empty scene behind, and felt a familiar nausea descend. It would be light for hours still, and she would be here burning through the window.

She didn't know any of the children who lived nearby. She didn't care normally: they all went to Cheatham Street School and looked inbred or violent. She was happy in her office with Mickey and her files. But sometimes on summer evenings she would watch groups of maybe thirty or forty children playing together. She knew the games now, she'd watched long enough. There were ones she had played at school, like British Bulldog and rounders, but the one that interested her was the one they called Jailer: some strange, estate-wide version of hide and seek, with cans being kicked, prisoners released and no apparent limits. She had once sat riveted to the window as she watched the search party fan the estate for the last boy hiding. He had held out for two hours, and the whole time Kate could see him quite clearly on the roof of the maisonettes. As the light faded and the searchers shouted his name with less and less patience, he had spotted his opportunity, jumped onto the stairwell roof and leapt unbelievably from there onto one of the sapling trees, which bent under his weight, dropping him on the ground right by the can, which he kicked to release the prisoners. Kate joined in the squeals of delight and laughter. She had even put on her coat to run out and join them, but she lost her nerve at the door.

Today the rain kept everyone behind glass. Kate pulled herself away from the window and forced herself to do some work.

Kate loved her room. Her grandmother had let her redecorate it after her dad died. Accordingly the carpet had been replaced with black and white checkered linoleum. Her old white melamine wardrobe, vanity table and drawers had been replaced with four second-hand filing cabinets along one wall. Her flimsy child's desk had been replaced with a large second-hand solid wood desk with drawers down one side, and best of all there had still been money for a swivel chair. Kate arranged the desk so that she sat facing the door with her back to the window. As instructed by *How to be a Detective*, she placed an angled mirror above her door so that from her desk she could still see all that went on in the street, and in particular would be aware of any attempts by bogus window cleaners to see her notes. It was hard to resist flying across the lino on her wheeled swivel chair, but after one afternoon spent doing little else, Kate now tried to keep a tight rein on this habit. She allowed herself ten scheduled minutes a day of chair fun, but beyond that all movement in the chair had to be purely functional. Sometimes she'd turn to get a pen from a drawer and she'd pretend not to notice that she had let the chair swing around too far – it was hard not to cheat a little like this – but in general no flagrant swivels or spins occurred outside the prescribed slot.

On the desk was Kate's typewriter, which she had received for Christmas when she was seven. Although it was only a child's plastic model, she found it did the job and didn't think clients would have any problem with this. She did, however, regret the stickers of ponies and dogs that she had stuck to the body of the typewriter that same Christmas; Sam Spade had never done that. Also on the desk was a small card file where she intended to keep names and details of contacts. So far only three out of the two hundred cards were filled in. One was for her next-door neighbour Adrian, one was for the local police station and one was for the DVLA. She had seen many detectives in American films check out people's licences and 'run checks on plates'. She wasn't sure how this worked in the UK, but she got the Swansea address out of a phone directory to save time, just in case.

This afternoon she was engaged in making her new

Identi-flick book. She had made her original one about eighteen months ago, closely following the instructions in *How to be a Detective*. The book had thirty pages and each page was cut into four horizontal strips. On the top strip of each page Kate had drawn a variety of haircuts, on the second strip eyebrows, eyes and tops of noses, on the third strip noses, and on the bottom strip chins and mouths. Kate had been fairly happy with the results, though she found that limitations in her drawing style had meant that at least half of the possible faces looked very similar: variations on Arthur Mullard. But now she was thinking bigger. The idea of placing an ad on the bus had made her critically reassess her office and her equipment, and she realized that much of it might fail to impress potential paying clients. Having an Identi-flick book was good and would certainly be a big help to any client trying to describe suspects, but Kate thought maybe a hand-drawn one would look unprofessional to some. So today she was redoing the book, but – and here was the master stroke – using cut up photos from magazines. Kate had an enormous pile of magazines on her desk that Adrian had saved for her, and she started patiently going through and cutting out any pages that had good clear headshots of a similar size.

As the afternoon wore on, the rain stopped, children were heard shouting across the estate again and Kate concentrated hard on the faces of strangers.

8

It was another barely breathing afternoon in Junior Three. Kate was looking out of the window at the maisonettes opposite where three mad dogs were terrorizing anyone who tried to walk across the scrappy patch of green and litter. Kate was frightened of dogs, though as she'd been bitten eleven times she couldn't see that it was an irrational fear. The estate was full of dogs – people bought them to make their lives safer, but it didn't work out that way. All the dogs had psychological problems: hatred of children, hatred of bikes, hatred of paperboys, hatred of black kids, hatred of white kids, hatred of fast-moving objects; some hated the sky and barked and leapt at it all day. The happy thing for the dogs was that there was always another dog who shared their psychosis and who they could join in a gang. The estate was patrolled by these packs of like-minded dogs, wandering the walkways and quads like incontinent, limping support groups. Kate stared out at their lolling tongues and their evil mouths and tried to keep calm. Dog owners would see her start to run away from their slavering, straining, ultra-violent beasts and would shout after her: 'Don't be scared, they smell fear.' This advice was supposed to be useful in a way that Kate couldn't understand. The other thing she couldn't grasp was the difference between a nip and a bite – she thought it was something to do with intent – but it was hard to tell. Six of the eleven times she'd been bitten, the dog's owner had been present at the scene, and in each case had said of the attack: 'He's only playing. It's a nip, not a bite.'

Kate watched as Mrs Byrne, the thinnest woman in the world, now struggled past the dogs with her double pushchair and multiple shopping bags. She thought there was something wrong with Mrs Byrne, something very sad, something to do with her lack of visibility. The dogs didn't bother with her; they looked straight through her as if she wasn't there. Mrs Byrne's daughter Karen was in Kate's class and she had once invited her back to her house for tea. Kate had noticed then that even her own children seemed to barely see Mrs Byrne. She was just a shadow, nervously darting from one room to the next. The carpets were all sticky in the flat and there was no Mr Byrne. Kate thought perhaps after unsticking his shoes from the carpet one day, he didn't fancy being stuck again and he'd left poor Mrs Byrne still attached to the swirling pattern underfoot.

The jarring scrape of metal chair on classroom floor brought Kate reluctantly back to the books in front of her. It was 2.45 on Tuesday afternoon. Tuesday and Thursday afternoons were maths – all afternoon, maths. Or they were once. About three months ago they had ceased to be maths classes and become the stagnant ponds of despair and hopelessness that they remained today. Back then in February, Kate had reached page 31 of *NumberWorx Maths* Book 4. Here she encountered for the first time the concept of angles and bearings. *NumberWorx Maths* had chosen to illustrate the topic with a picture story involving an air traffic control tower, and various aeroplanes vying for landing spots. Kate had studied the page for a long time. She had plenty of time: she and Paddy Hurley were two books clear of the rest of the class. So she took her time trying to understand the little raised circle symbols, the dotted lines, the seemingly random numbers. They made no sense, but she was in no hurry to ask Mrs Finnegan.

An hour or so passed in which Kate explored various possible interpretations of the data. She had covered a side of paper with increasingly knotted and frayed calculations when Paddy Hurley tapped on her elbow and indicated that he too was stuck on page 31. They sat whispering and exchanging proposed ways forward, until at 2.55 p.m., after losing the toss, Kate had raised her hand and requested Mrs Finnegan's attention.

Now it was three months later. Kate and Paddy were still on page 31, but the difference was so was the rest of the class. Only last week, Mark McGrath, the slowest boy in the class, had staggered and stumbled blindly to the fateful page only to trip over the pile of bodies waiting there for him.

Mrs Finnegan, though criminally unsuited to teaching small children, was in fact a very fine mathematician. On that first day when Kate had asked for her assistance with page 31, Mrs Finnegan believed she had given as clear and precise an explanation of angles and bearings as she could. But sadly neither Kate or Paddy had understood a word of the graduate-level lecture she delivered. Over the subsequent weeks more and more children would raise their hands and ask about page 31, and every time her perfect explanation was greeted with blank faces something died inside Mrs Finnegan, until finally she gave up. For the last two months anyone foolish enough to venture that they were stuck on page 31 was told in a dead voice: 'Well, unstick yourself.' Occasionally a brighter, more thick-skinned child might think they had cracked the mystery and would suggest their inevitably flawed interpretation of the data to Mrs Finnegan, who would stare coldly at them until they trailed off into silence.

Kate was turning over in her head the pros and cons of

a walkie-talkie system for the agency. The pros were obvious – walkie talkies were amazing, without any competition the most amazingly brilliant things in the world. Kate could not be in a shop that sold walkie-talkie kits without staring at the boxes for at least half an hour, and during that time she'd feel a kind of manic excitement. She'd look at the pictures on the box that showed a kid holding the walkie talkie and zigzag lines coming out of the earpiece – suggesting static crackle, suggesting sound waves, suggesting magic – and then some equally jagged writing saying 'Can you read me? Over.' Kate would swoon. She thought about having a walkie-talkie system the way other girls might dream about having a pony. The cons were equally obvious – Mickey couldn't speak, and couldn't hold things; he'd be useless with a walkie talkie. It would not be magic, it would be an inert lump of plastic she'd have to sellotape to his head. Kate sighed and then did a double take as she saw Teresa was looking at page 63 in *NumberWorx Maths*. She'd avoided speaking to Teresa ever since Teresa had given up on her classmates altogether and decided to conduct all her business with them in burp language, but she was provoked by the sight of Teresa sullying the distant paradise of page 63 with her crazy presence.

'Mrs Finnegan said none of us were allowed to skip page 31. We have to unstick ourselves before we can move past it.'

Teresa looked at her with a furrowed brow for a couple of seconds, but then gave up trying to understand and went back to her book.

Kate tried again: 'Teresa – you can't just do any page you like, you have to work through the book in order. I'd be on page 100 or something now if I'd done that.'

Teresa looked up, more annoyed this time. 'Yeah, but you couldn't, could you? Because you're stuck on some page which she won't explain. I don't need her – she can't tell me nothing.'

'She'll find out you've skipped it and then she'll shout for hours and hours.'

'How would she find out? She hasn't left her desk in months. She's a broken thing. I watched her break. She shouts now but it's not like before, she got broken. Anyway, I didn't skip anything. It's easy.'

Kate sat for a while trying hard not to rise to this bait, knowing it was going to be a prelude to some new horror from Teresa, but she caved in. 'Show me what you did on page 31.'

Teresa flicked back through her workbook and Kate steeled herself for a page covered in rude drawings, or maybe even smeared in poo – she really put nothing past Teresa. Instead she was presented with a neatly completed page, along with some workings out and notes in the margins.

Kate stared at the page trying to see what stupid mistakes Teresa had made, and as she looked Teresa started: 'If you just imagine a circle is a cake that has been cut up into 360 slices . . .' And over the next twenty minutes Teresa delivered a clear, wide-ranging monologue that explained perfectly everything Kate might want to know about angles and bearings and other key concepts of trigonometry.

9

Monday morning of half term and Kate had called a meeting with Mickey to rethink Falcon Investigations' strategy. She was beginning to doubt if anything truly big was ever going to happen at Green Oaks and she worried how the agency was going to make a name for itself. She allowed herself to spin round and round in the swivel chair to help her think. Mickey watched from his position, leaned against the typewriter.

'We need to solve a crime, Mickey, that's what detectives do,' Kate said, before sinking into thought again. Putting in the hours was essential, but a good investigator had to rely on instinct too. Kate's instinct had always told her that something serious would happen at Green Oaks, something she could make a name for herself with, but now she worried that maybe her instinct was wrong.

She looked through her notebooks and found the Green Oaks material thin – suspicion, surmise, but no real suspects, no evidence, no crime. Maybe, given the security presence and all the cameras there, Falcon Investigations was wasting its time.

Wrong place, wrong time – these words haunted her.

Perhaps there were richer pickings in the local neighbourhood. Maybe crime was on her doorstep and she was walking past it every day. She was always alert, she made notes on the neighbourhood when she spent time there – but maybe now it was time to switch the agency's resources.

After another hour's chair-spinning Kate had a proposal. Falcon Investigations would focus 50–50 on the local area and Green Oaks over the next four weeks. At the end of that period notes would be reviewed thoroughly and the agency would then focus one hundred per cent on whichever location seemed the more potentially criminal.

Day one of the new strategy couldn't have started off better. One of Mr Palmer's paperboys phoned in sick and Kate begged him to let her do the afternoon round instead. This was a golden opportunity to do some real, upclose surveillance work in the neighbourhood. Mr Palmer was dubious: Kate was too young for the job and he wasn't sure it was work for a girl, but with Adrian laid up with the same bug he didn't have a lot of choice.

She squeezed Mickey alongside all the copies of the *Evening Mail* in the big delivery bag and set off, weaving slightly under its weight. She delivered first to a row of council houses. Every one of them had a small front garden, and every one was pristine and ornamented with individual personal touches. One had a bench, one had a wishing well, one had a red-faced gnome fishing from a puddle-sized pond. The sun beat down and the smell of hot creosote filled the air. As she walked up each path Kate tried to deduce as much as she could about the people inside from the clues around her. The first house had a sign on the door saying 'Never mind the dog, beware of the wife', and Kate made a mental note to remember that some kind of deranged person lived there. The second house had another sign which Kate looked at for a long time, but could make no sense of it: 'No hawkers, No canvassers'. In the end she copied it down in her notebook. She thought 'hawkers' might be some kind of big bird – maybe the owner didn't want them eating the flowers or the cat.

The fourth house had added a porch. The porch door

had no letter box and after a few moments' puzzling Kate realized that she had to open the outer door to gain access to the original inner door where the letter box was. She couldn't see the point of this. She couldn't understand how the owners, once embarked on this extra door policy, knew when to stop. She imagined front door after front door extending all the way up the garden path, with delivery people having to pass through each one before finally reaching the letter box. She opened the white plastic outer door and found the small area inside to be filled with shoes and coats. She shook her head slowly and said aloud to Mickey: 'These are the people who need us, Mickey. Unlocked door plus possessions equals crime.' She made a note to put a Falcon Investigations card through the door when she'd had them printed.

As she made her way along the row of houses she came across more and more porches. Each one was its own little world, rich with clues about the owners. Some had neat tables and flower arrangements, some were filled with Victorian dolls, some contained a tangle of children's bikes and roller-skates, others smelled of tomato soup. Kate was having to stop and make notes in her pad at each one. She jotted down deductions about the owners and decided she'd read them to Adrian when he was back at work to see how close she was. She was particularly keen to share with him her conviction that number 32 was a kidnapper, as evidenced by the cut up newspapers and duct tape in the porch. When the row of houses came to an end she looked at her digital watch and was shocked to see she had taken an hour and a half delivering to just thirty houses. She hurried on.

Next stop was Trafalgar House, a twenty-storey block of flats that stood apart from the other high-rise blocks like a sentry guarding the entrance to the estate. The building cast a shadow over Kate's school playground, and over the years from different classrooms she had learned to tell the time just from which parts of the playground were sunny and which weren't. She remembered a strange short-lived cult back when she was in Infant One, when everyone in the class fervently believed a ghost lived in one of the flats on the twentieth floor. They would crouch down on the concrete every breaktime and squint up at the distant window, where no curtains were, and occasionally a classmate would scream and say they'd seen the ghost and everyone would scatter all over the playground. Kate never saw it. Even aged five she wasn't sure she believed in ghosts, but she kept watching anyway. She preferred it to skipping, which was all the other girls seemed to do at break.

Despite the shadow it cast over her, Kate had never been inside Trafalgar House. Now she passed by the deserted playground set in front of it, where she liked to hang from the climbing frame and think sometimes. It was always cold in the playground, which was held deep in the shadow of the block, buffeted by cross winds swirling around the tower. She reached the front door and pressed the button that said 'Trades' just as Mr Palmer had instructed. The door buzzed and Kate pushed her way into the dark interior. The lobby had two lifts and was filled with a smell that she had never smelled before. It was a bit like a swimming pool, a bit like an empty classroom. It was a sad smell.

Mr Palmer had arranged the papers so that Kate would start at the top of the block and work her way down the stairs to each floor. Kate pressed the button for the lift and soon the little black window turned to a dim yellow and the door opened. The lift wasn't like the shiny glass lifts at Green Oaks; it was battered metal inside and covered with names and words. Kate was disappointed. She remembered a children's programme she used to watch with her dad when she was very young. A girl lived in a block of flats with her pet mouse and dog. Every day she'd get in the lift and the mouse would jump on the dog's nose to press the button for the right floor. Kate loved that. She used to wish she lived in a block of flats with a lift. But now as she tried to keep her feet out of the puddle in the corner and looked at the cigarette burns on the lift buttons, she thought maybe the girl wasn't so lucky after all.

She worked her way down each of the block's twenty floors and she didn't see a single living thing. The clues she could gather about the people who lived there were limited to the waft of food smells and TV sounds that issued from each letter box as she lifted it. No one put flowers or gnomes outside their front doors here. No one seemed to use their front doors at all. She wondered if they ever left their big cuboid tower or if they spent their days waiting for deliveries from 'Trades' like Kate. She imagined people picking up the newspapers she dropped through their doors, reading about a world they never visited. For the first time it occurred to her that her classmates had been right. Except it wasn't just one ghost, but many, one in every flat. Floating through the walls, communicating only through the strange words and symbols they left in the lift.

Out in the sunlight again, Kate walked over to the maisonettes where the rest of the papers were going. The contrast with Trafalgar House was striking. People sat out on the hillocks of grass between the blocks and children played. Kate recognized some of the children from school and felt self-conscious as she walked past them with her bag. She exchanged smiles or waves, but felt unable to get out her pad and carry on taking notes on the things she saw. She gently pushed Mickey further down in the bag, out of view. She realized that was one of the things she really liked about Green Oaks – nobody knew her. She wasn't the quiet girl from class. She wasn't the girl with no mom or dad. She was a detective, an invisible operative gliding through the malls, seeing things no one else noticed.

Lost in thoughts about crime, Kate didn't notice the three dogs that had followed her into the quiet quadrangle she was cutting across. It was only when one started growling that she turned around to see them, tongues lolling, eyes fixed on her. She told herself not to show fear, but the message got to her legs too late and she was already running away as fast as she could. The dogs followed, barking madly. Kate was being slowed by the bag and without giving it too much thought she pulled Mickey out and threw the newspapers behind her. The dogs stopped momentarily to sniff the bag, giving Kate a few moments' lead to run faster than she ever had before, just reaching the waste area at the bottom of one of the blocks and pulling the door shut behind her before the dogs slammed into it, jumping up and growling furiously. She hugged Mickey tightly as she leaned against the foul-smelling bin and looked out of the slatted doors at the dogs. She couldn't seem to breathe fast enough. Her chest hurt and tears stung her eyes. Wrong place, wrong time, she thought.

She nuzzled her face into Mickey's soft head and whispered breathlessly in his ears: 'Change of strategy: all resources back to Green Oaks.'

10

In the following months Adrian and Kate would spend the dead newsagent hours between lunchtime rush and evening paper constructing lurid tales about the customers. They liked to paste the colourful characters and plot details from famous crime movies onto the pastel anorak forms of the local pensioners who came in daily for their Herbal Tablets and *People's Friend*s.

Adrian: Have you noticed that Mrs Dale hasn't been in for some days now?

Kate: What are you thinking?

Adrian: Well, Mr Dale, whilst buying a quarter of troach drops in here yesterday, was witnessed to be carrying what appeared to be a very heavy suitcase.

Kate: !

Adrian: Exactly. When questioned as to the wellbeing of his wife, the aforementioned Mrs Dale, Mr Dale replied – get this – 'She's staying at her sister's in Yarmouth.'

Kate: They always say that!

Adrian: Funny, isn't it? We've never heard of this 'sister' before – or 'Yarmouth'.

Kate: That's more than funny. That's fishy.

Adrian: Exactly what I thought. So I said, casually of course, 'And yourself, Mr Dale, you're not joining your wife?'

Kate: Good one, Adrian.

Adrian: Yeah, I thought so.

Kate: So what did he say?

Adrian: He said, 'Yes, I'm off there right now, hence the suitcase. I've just come in to cancel the papers.'

Kate (after a pause): He's clever, isn't he?

Adrian: Diabolical.

Kate: Cancel the wife then cancel the papers. Cold-Blooded Mr Dale.

They called Mr Jackson of 42 Showell Gardens 'The Ruthless Assassin' because he wore a natty car coat and had leather gloves. Mr Porlock, who stopped his Jag outside every morning to call in and pick up his paper, was 'The Gentleman Embezzler' on account of being the only customer to buy the *Financial Times*. Kelvin O'Reilly from Cheatham Street was 'The Henchman' because he was big and not very bright.

Anyone who asked for chocolate limes was a killer, according to Adrian, due to his abhorrence of the sweet and his belief that no law-abiding person could like such an unnatural combination. 'They've stepped outside the norms of society, Kate. Their moral compass has gone crazy. Anything goes.' In addition Adrian referred sinisterly to anyone who bought plain chocolate as 'One with dark appetites'.

Kate tried to base her suspicions on more concrete evidence, but even she couldn't help feeling dubious of anyone who bought prawn cocktail crisps. They both agreed, though, that Kit Kat buyers were generally forces for good in society.

Adrian usually had a late lunch around three p.m. when Mr Palmer had finished his. If Kate was off school and the weather was fine they'd go for a walk down to the canal. Despite the setting being more fitting for the topic, they rarely spoke of murder or crime outside the shop.

One day Kate asked Adrian: 'Will you leave the shop? Will you get a job in town one day?'

'I dunno. Maybe. I try not to think about it.'

'But your dad would always need help, wouldn't he? I mean he has to go the wholesaler's and do his books: who would look after the shop then?'

'Well, I think he'd like to get an assistant to help him out.'

'He wouldn't get your little sister in, would he?' Kate was slightly scared of Adrian's scowling, punkish sister.

Adrian laughed. 'I don't think she'd set foot in here. It's not her thing. She's too busy getting through vats of Boots Country Born Gel and cross-examining me about my musical tastes. I don't think he wants either of us to work here. He can't see why he spent all those years contributing to my education, for me to end up selling Polo mints.'

'But it's what he does.'

'Exactly.'

'Do you always do what your dad wants?'

Adrian sighed. 'No, not really. But it's his shop.'

'But in general do you think he knows what's best for you?'

'I don't know, Kate, I'm sorry. I don't really have any big ideas about it. I just drift along. I'm happy here, but he's not happy for me to be here.'

Kate threw a stone in the canal. 'I think sometimes adults . . . Well, I know you're an adult, but I mean dads or moms – or grandmothers – they think they know what's best for their children but they don't really. In fact often they have very bad ideas, and the children have much better ideas, but it doesn't matter because the grandmother, or whoever, is the adult and so they get to choose. Even if it might make the younger person really, really unhappy and miserable.'

Kate paused, as if she'd finished, but then started again, not looking Adrian in the eye. 'For example, here's an example, right . . .' Adrian could hear Kate's voice waver a little '. . . my grandmother, but I'm not supposed to call her that, I'm supposed to call her Ivy. Ivy says I have to go to Redspoon at the end of next year.'

'The boarding school?'

'Yeah. She says they have no-fees places for bright children – it's an opportunity, and that living with her isn't right for me. She says she can't look after me properly. So I tell her I don't need looking after. I can make spaghetti on toast. I can work the washing machine. And then she says I need to be with people my own age. But I don't like that.' Kate's voice broke a little. 'I don't really like being with people my own age so much. They don't do anything – they just watch telly . . . and . . . and I'm not sure they like me very much either because I'm not very fast at running and I think maybe some of them think I'm strange. I like it best when school finishes and I can do my detective work. I tried to tell her about it. I told her how I'm going to solve crimes, and that's what Dad wanted me to do. He wanted me to be a detective, not go to some stupid school away from home. Dad would never have sent me away from him . . .'

Adrian gave Kate a tissue, but still she didn't look at him.

'She says I shouldn't bother you in the shop. She says I'm a nuisance to you and that it's not natural to have no friends my own age. She says you probably feel sorry for me and think I'm very odd.'

Adrian knelt down and turned Kate's head so that she was looking at him. 'Don't listen to her, Kate. You're not a nuisance and you're not odd. You're my friend. I'd go mental in that shop in the afternoons on my own. You've got more about you than the rest of them. I admire you, Kate, I do. Look at me, I'm twenty-two and I do nothing. I'm going nowhere. You're ten and you're a little hive of industry, always running about, always with some project or scheme, always with stuff to do. You make the adults look dead. It doesn't matter how old you are, I'd be your friend if you were eighty-five or if you were twenty-five. You're burning brighter than the rest of us. She should be proud of you.'

They were both quiet for a few minutes.

Kate looked at Adrian and said, 'I'm not going to that school.'

11

Kate and Teresa sat on the concrete steps of Ramsey House. The pane of frosted glass in front of them was smashed and through it they had a clear view of Chattaway House's second-floor landing.

'Do you know about the ginger man at number 26?' Teresa asked.

Kate didn't know anything about anyone who lived in that block. Whenever Teresa spoke about her neighbours it was with an assumption that Kate naturally knew of them and their ways. Kate liked this.

'He is a trampy man. He has big ginger hair and a big ginger beard and he sits on the hill all day eating orange peel from a bag. He can tell the future. He tells me what will happen to me all the time. He knows all about you. He told me about you a long time ago.'

'What did he say?' Kate asked.

'He made me promise not to tell.'

Kate let this go. Conversations with Teresa were never straightforward. There were always riddles. Kate liked this too. 'Who lives next door to him?'

'An Irishman. His name is Vincent O'Hanorahan and he talks like this: "Odelodelodelodelodelodel". You have to shut your eyes to understand what he's saying and he wears trousers too small for him. I've been in his flat. He was at his window and waved me to come in. I went in and he gave me a biscuit covered in pink mallow and coconut, but he didn't call it a biscuit, he called it Kimberley. I told him that was a girl's name and he said he'd never met a girl called Kimberley and then he asked me my name. He had pictures of Mary and Jesus everywhere and his kitchen smelled of mud. I told him my name was Teresa and he started to cry. He cried and cried with his head on the table. I finished eating the biscuit and then I left.'

Kate stared at Teresa. She had no idea how much of what Teresa said was true and how much was made up. She'd started to think that it all might be true. She'd started to think that nothing normal ever happened to Teresa. She looked back across at the landing. 'Look – they're watching television in that one.' She was amazed anyone could be watching TV on such a sunny day.

'That's Mr and Mrs Franks. They're the oldest people in the block. Mrs Franks has the television on top volume all day long. She sits in a big knitted blanket that she knitted herself with lots of coloured squares. Mr Franks told me she knitted it when she was younger. He said he never knew why she was knitting it. Sometimes Mr Franks talks to me and gives me 10p for sweets and tells me I'm a good girl. He smiles at me with a nice smile and his eyes go watery. Other times he calls me a dirty blackie and a filthy half-breed and he tells me to clear off back to the jungle.'

Kate and Teresa looked at each other and then burst out laughing.

Much to Mrs Finnegan's horror, Kate and Teresa had started to get along. Ever since the *NumberWorx Maths* episode, Kate had started to see a different side to Teresa. She'd begun to see how bored Teresa was in class, how she always knew the answer but never put her hand up. How she sat with a vacant look on her face, doodling while others in the class volunteered wrong answer after wrong answer. She saw how Mrs Finnegan looked at her as if she was something she'd trodden in. She almost began to understand why Teresa acted so crazily.

At first Kate had been a little cynical. When she had realized that Teresa wasn't a total lunatic, she invited her back to her house for tea. She thought that maybe if Ivy saw her with the much-demanded friend of her own age, then she might not feel she had to go to Redspoon. But Teresa had strange stories and mad ideas and she seemed to wander about on her own as much as Kate did. Kate didn't show her the office, or tell her about the agency . . . but she thought she might do one day. She'd noticed that Teresa was brilliant at surveillance.

The steps were getting too uncomfortable to sit on so they moved off out into the warm afternoon sun. Someone was playing Althea & Donna and the sound echoed across the empty streets. They walked over the grass expanses between the flats, past the climbing frame where a small child was stuck and crying for help.

They walked away from the estate, over the railway bridge and alongside an old, crumbling brick wall. After a few hundred yards they came to a small green door in the wall and they walked through into St Joseph's graveyard. The church and grounds were set on a steep slope. The church was halfway down, approached by a winding path from the top or a drive from the bigger gates at the bottom. Stretched out on all sides of the church were the graves, scattered randomly on the slopes – many of them now toppled or leaning madly in the long grass and weeds.

The graves were all old, dating from the turn of the century up until the 1950s. The only new ones were in a small plot behind the presbytery reserved for children of the parish. Standing out from the other ivied and furred-over headstones, these monuments were gleaming black or white marble, with gold inscriptions and smiling images of the dead children in little ovals. There were always fresh flowers on these graves, along with stone teddy bears and faded dolls. Among them was the grave of Wayne West, a boy Kate remembered vaguely from Infants One, who had somehow put his head inside a plastic bag and suffocated. Every year he was remembered in prayers at school and in mass, but Kate always wondered if he had really died in that way. It seemed such a convenient cautionary tale. Kate was waiting for the day that the teachers would present some blind boy in assembly who had lost his vision when someone had thrown a snowball with a stone in it. The school had already had a talk from a boy with one foot who had lost the other playing on the railway tracks. Kate had a gruesome image of teachers from competing schools bidding for injured children at the local hospital and ascribing a range of childhood misdemeanours to them. 'I've got a paraplegic little girl here, ideal for stamping out leaning back on chairs.' 'This almost-blind boy, ideal for carrot promotion.'

It seemed that Teresa spent a lot of her time at the graveyard. She loved the weather-beaten brick wall that cut the place off from the outside world. The church and surrounding graves were the same age as the block of houses where Kate lived. They formed another little island surrounded on all sides by the new cul-de-sacs and passages of the estate. But in the churchyard no one would disturb you. No one ever visited during the week. The priest would come and go in his beaten up Volvo but he never noticed Teresa sitting in the shade of the wall studying the dried filigree skeletons of dead leaves.

Today they sat under a horse chestnut tree next to the gravestone of the Kearney family. The parents and three children had all died in the same fire in 1914. They were survived by the youngest girl, Muriel, who had lived on until 1957. She was fondly remembered by her loving husband William, but of him there was no sign. Teresa got up and walked over to a bush, where she started pulling off small red berries.

‘Don’t eat those,’ said Kate. ‘They could be poisonous.’

‘They are poisonous,’ replied Teresa, ‘but they don’t kill you in small portions. I’m not going to eat them.’

‘Why are you picking them?’

‘Because they give you a wicked stomach ache and make your gums burn.’

Kate waited for more explanation, but Teresa just carried on picking the berries and putting them in the pocket of her shorts.

After some thought Kate asked: ‘Is it to get the day off school?’

‘I go to school when I want. I can come and sit here any day.’ When she’d filled her pockets, Teresa sat down next to Kate and tugged at the grass nearby. ‘It’s for my dad – he’s not my dad, but I have to call him my dad. I like making things for him.’

‘What sort of things?’ Kate asked.

‘Things that hurt him. Things that make him ill. Things that keep him in bed and away from us. Away from my mom. He says to me, “Get me a drink of something, I’m dying of thirst here.” So I go and make him a nice refreshing cup of Lift – the lemon tea drink that lifts you up. He loves that stuff. He likes it with lots of sugar – “hot lemonade” cos he’s such a baby. So I put one heaped teaspoon of Lift, two heaped teaspoons of lemon Flash floor cleaner and three heaped teaspoons of sugar and he drinks it up like he hasn’t had water for months.’

‘You’re poisoning him!’ Kate burst out.

‘I’m not poisoning him. I’m checking him. Once a month or so I like to check him. Keep him in his room. Give us a break. He loves jam on his cake. He has it for breakfast. Half a swiss-roll covered in extra jam. He calls me from his bed: “Where’s my breakfast, girl?” So now I can give him extra berries in his extra jam.’

‘But isn’t he very ill?’

'We can hear him crying out from the bedroom, rolling around holding his fat gut, and we turn the telly up. Mom takes him to the doctor, and the doctor says he has a peptic ulcer, says it's the drink. The doctor's stupid – the doctor wants him gone – the doctor hates the estate. Mom says, "Please, Carl, I beg you, don't drink. You're killing yourself. What will we do without you?" So he punches her in the face and he breaks her ribs, and I make him something else.'

Kate said nothing for a while. Then she said, 'You won't kill him, will you? Cos they'll find out. The detectives would know. They have forensic people and they'd do a post-mortem and they'd find the evidence. They'd know it was murder. You'd get sent away.'

'I like it here: it's quiet and safe and no one bothers me. But when I'm at home I have the telly up loud and all I can think about is how to get away. My sister got away. My mom never will. I have to get out of there. I've been hiding and sneaking and keeping out of his reach – he hasn't had the chance for months – but I know he wants to, and if he beats me up again, I'll kill him and then I'll push his body into the rubbish chute and send it down to the big bin.'

12

TOP SECRET. DETECTIVE NOTEBOOK.
PROPERTY OF AGENT KATE MEANEY.

Friday 24th August
Surveillance on bus impossible due to having 'Mad Alan' sat next to me. He showed me his collection of bus tickets (all for the number 43) and asked me if I believed in Christ the Redeemer. I told him there wasn't enough evidence.

Saw woman with empty pushchair again. Today she was by the play area.

Saturday 25th August
Adrian let me test out new tape recorder in the shop. Sound quality variable – clarity difficult through my canvas bag where it is concealed. Have fairly clear recordings of Mrs Hall asking for Spot the Ball coupon and Mr Vickers getting angry about dog mess on the estate, then a long spell of unclear dialogue with only the words 'he won't tolerate mallow' audible. Not sure it will pick up much at Green Oaks.

Sunday 26th August
Tall man with limp acting suspiciously at rear of Mr and Mrs Evans'.

Saw him standing outside back gate for 20 minutes before calling 'Shirley' repeatedly up to back window in loud whisper. Mrs Evans appeared at window and threw down keys to man – who let himself in back door. No further sightings. Adrian advised not telling Mr Evans . . . he said it's an affair!

Monday 27th August
Visited Mr Watkin the butcher in the afternoon. Observed that Mr Watkin sniffs meat when no customers are in shop – any meat that makes his nose wrinkle is put at the front of the counter. Mr Watkin saw me looking and explained 'stock rotation' to me – very interesting.

Tuesday 28th August
Went to cemetery today. Told Dad about work. Very quiet at cemetery. No surveillance.

Wednesday 29th August
Back in Mr Watkin's – but very few customers again. Noticed similarity in packaging of rat poison that Mr Watkin keeps hidden behind the counter and the packaging of the seasoning for his 'special cutlets'. Further noticed that Mr Watkin seems slightly short-sighted (initially thought I was Mrs Khan) – now very worried that Mr Watkin may commit manslaughter.

Thursday 30th August
Swarthy squat woman stood outside H. Samuel Green Oaks branch today for 45 minutes looking in window. Just window shopping?

Friday 31st August
Told Adrian of Mr Watkin worries, but he said that no one ever bought meat from him any more so not to worry. Adrian said the shop was more of a hobby for Mr Watkin. He said that sometimes Mrs Watkin will ask her friends to come in and buy something but she gives them the money

back secretly and tells them to put the meat straight in the bin. Conspiracies on my own doorstep.

Saturday 1st September
Green Oaks: two hours outside the banks today. Nothing to note except short man walking about unaware of 4 foot length of toilet paper stuck to his shoes.

Sunday 2nd September
Spotted suspicious male loitering in Sainsbury's car park – not clear what his intention was.

13

Kate had learned something about Teresa which amazed her: Teresa couldn't discern any hierarchy of naughtiness at school. She understood that certain acts were deemed bad, but the relationship between these acts was impossible for her to guess at. It took much time and much trial and error for any scale of badness to become apparent to her.

She had learned that reacting in any way to the school bell was wrong. Teresa used to kick back her chair and flee the classroom as soon as she heard the bell, running blindly out into the surprised empty playground. This had been incorrect. Apparently the bell was there to tell the teacher the time, not to signal playtime to pupils. Teresa thought it would be easier for the teacher to look at their watch, or the big ticking clock at the front of the classroom, but now she knew that preparing her escape had to be done much more subtly and slowly: books gradually slid off the desk into the waiting bag, watching the teacher attentively all the while. Kate had helped her and now she had learned this. But even now, as Kate and Teresa began their final year at St Joseph's, she still hadn't learned that reacting to the bell was a lesser misdemeanour than, for example, carving her name on the desk or putting worms in Darren Wall's pink blancmange pudding.

So it was after a great deal of hapless research and unwitting pushing of boundaries that Teresa finally stumbled upon the naughtiest thing to do at school. One dark stormy lunchtime, when the rain kept the children confined to indoor play, Teresa rounded a corner too quickly and discovered the truth. In the seemingly endless aftermath, Teresa became aware that running with scissors was the greatest act of evil, and running with scissors that then somehow collided disastrously with the thigh of the head teacher was off the scale of outrage.

News spread fast around the steaming classrooms, but rumours spread faster. Within minutes of impact wild stories were being relayed. Teresa Stanton had an axe. Teresa Stanton was stabbing everyone. Teresa Stanton had murdered the headmaster and was going to kill the rest of the teachers. The children, incapable of processing such explosive gossip, could only run around in circles or jump up and down wildly, like dogs in a storm.

In the first of many assemblies on the incident, the true, modest extent of the accident was reluctantly revealed. Mr Woods had narrowly escaped any serious injury, but a very good pair of House of Fraser trousers had been 'slashed beyond repair'. Kate, as something of an expert in the field, was very unimpressed with the forensic evidence offered. Mr Woods held the trousers up for the pupils to squint at the small pull in the fabric, and as he slowly moved them around for all to see he repeated solemnly: 'Imagine if this had been your face,' sometimes adding a name for personalized effect: 'Yes, Karen, imagine. Your face.'

Teresa was mystified. She couldn't believe that she'd be punished for something that was an accident, she couldn't understand what purpose punishment would serve.

Kate knew that Mr Woods would make an example of Teresa. After a special meeting of the PTA it was announced that she would be suspended for a week. The weather was rotten and so Teresa couldn't spend her days in the churchyard. Kate thought of Teresa stuck inside the thin-walled box of her maisonette with her step-father, plotting ways to silence him and, more than ever, Kate wanted to avert a crime.

14

The climbing frame was a tubular metal igloo. The metal had rusted in parts and when the wind blew, as it did today, the rushing air found empty screw holes and fissures in the frame and played a sad tune on the pipes. Kate loved the sound. It helped her think. She hung upside down from the centre of the igloo, her hair dangling on the red concrete below. Crisp packets and carrier bags blew around the edges of the play area, and the wind carried the smell of boiled vegetables from the flats mixed with an industrial metallic smell from the factories.

She was back in the small playground in the shadow of Trafalgar House and she let her eyes travel down past the door of the block, past hundreds of balconies, past scraps of washing, past plastic tractor bikes and rotting kitchen cupboards, past the tangle of aerials, down far below to where white clouds were moving across the pale blue motorway of the sky. If her legs lost their grip she'd plunge for miles and miles and then eventually hit the cushion of a cloud. She watched them motor by and thought about the suspect she'd seen at Green Oaks.

Kate spotted him after school on Monday, as soon as she'd turned the corner and walked towards the banks. She was sure he was the same man who had been sitting there the other day. She hadn't seen him properly then, but she'd sensed a certain posture and she saw it again now. She had always known that she would see something different in the face and as she drew closer she felt a thrill of recognition as his features became clearer. The man was looking across the children's play area towards the branch of Lloyds Bank. Kate watched discreetly from the doorway of a building society. The man looked like he was trying to act normal; Kate recognized the signs, she did it herself whenever she worked surveillance. He sat awkwardly, he looked at his watch, his eyes flicked about; he didn't look blank. Kate carefully walked in a wide arc so that she was positioned on a distant bench behind the man. This was a suspect, and in the place where she had always known one would appear. She was calm because she was ready. She knew now that the hard work would begin. Primarily a lot of surveillance. She needed to piece together a coherent picture of the suspect's plan. Was he working alone? Doubtful, Kate had originally thought: solo bank jobs were rushed, desperate affairs, with no planning. He looked too cool for that. Was this an initial staking of the joint, or was the heist near maturity? Kate didn't know but she felt these were early days, she'd been watching the banks for so long and knew she'd only seen this man once before. The question was: how long did she have?

She'd been watching him every day since then. He always sat outside the banks between four and five – just before they closed. Kate would get the slow bus to Green Oaks straight from school. She'd sit on her favourite watching bench eating the peanut butter sandwiches she packed in the morning, and after a few minutes he'd show up. It was hard to tell which bank was the target. It seemed to be Lloyds. He made no notes and he took no photos. He was too professional to do anything so conspicuous. Kate realized now that he was working on his own – there was no sign of a gang or an accomplice.

An ice-cream van passed by somewhere on the estate. 'Greensleeves' tinkled out and then stopped abruptly. She tried to picture his face in her mind. She had been disappointed to find that her home-made Identi-flick book was entirely useless when presented with a real challenge. The first day she'd got a really good look at him she had rushed home to try and capture the image through slashes of other people's faces. The best result looked nothing like him. The best result looked like nothing on earth. The only thing that had cheered her up was that the professional Identikit images shown on *Police Five* didn't look much better. Kate thought that if anyone with those faces walked the streets, zookeepers would be called in to shoot them with tranquillizer darts.

Kate intended to take her dad's camera next time, but in the meantime she'd tried the old fall-back of a drawing – or, as *How to be a Detective* inevitably called them, 'Identi-sketches'.

Study your suspect closely. Jot down words to describe him. If possible, make a sketch. Is he fat or thin, tall or short, smart or shabby? Does he have any distinguishing features? Make a note of the clothes he is wearing – but remember: clothes may be changed, moustaches may be false, hair may be cut. Successful criminals are masters of disguise. (Kate had underlined this last sentence.)

But there was something about the eyes that she found too difficult. His eyes were somehow frightening and impossible to remember at the same time. Back in her office she'd said to Mickey: 'I don't like the look of his eyes. What do you reckon?'

Mickey was as circumspect as usual.

'I think there's violence there.'

Mickey stared ahead grimly.

'A killer? Well, it wouldn't be the first time. We know that solo bank robbers are ruthless operatives.'

Mickey and Kate had been to the library to do some research. They had each been a little disconcerted by the number of bank robbers who killed. John Elgin Johnson, a lone bandit armed with a blue steel revolver. Charles Arthur 'Pretty Boy' Floyd and the Kansas City Massacre. George 'Baby Face' Nelson, the Baader-Meinhof Gang, the Symbionese Liberation Army . . . the list went on. They were uncomfortable with this information. In fact, they were distinctly unnerved by how different in tone the grown-up books on crime in the library were from the perky advice and images in *How to be a Detective*. Kate and Mickey's manual had quite a lot on disguises and secret codes but nothing about dealing with fanatical Red Army factions, nothing about gun-happy psychopaths, nothing about being doused in petrol and threatened with a lighter. Kate had a small twinge of doubt about exactly how true to life her book was.

Pins and needles were marching up her feet and so Kate sat up on the climbing frame and looked out over the estate. She realized that she and Mickey couldn't tackle the suspect on their own. She wanted to gather as much evidence and information as she could. Find out where he was staying, find out how he planned to get away. All robbers did a dry run first. She'd watch and wait and record all she saw. Then when the robbery finally happened, maybe she couldn't hand over the perpetrator, but she could hand over enough evidence to lead the police to him. She was sure that would be enough for the special post she dreamt of. Not a proper job, obviously: she'd still go to school, but maybe an occasional call for her assistance with tricky surveillance operations. The police would see her usefulness. How many other kids had her training? How many others were invisible like Kate seemed to be?

'Well, Kate, looks like your suspicions about unit 15

on the Langsdale Industrial Estate were well founded as always.'

'Diamond smuggling?'

'Exactly. An extensive ring covering all the hubs in the diamond industry: Cape Town, Amsterdam, the West Midlands. The problem is, Kate, we need to get a look inside that unit. We need photos of the packages actually on the premises. None of our men can get close. We've tried all the usual – gas meter readers, window cleaners, you name it – but these are smart cookies. They won't let anyone near the premises. They suspect everyone . . . except maybe . . .'

'A child?'

'Correct.'

Kate looked across at the cooling towers and saw her future stretched in front of her. Working in her office, taking lunch at Vanezi's with Mickey, telling Adrian about her cases, getting Teresa involved – and definitely no Redspoon.

2003

VOICES IN THE STATIC

15

He never expected to see anything on the CCTV. No one ever did on the night shift.

He'd been looking at the same monitor screens for the past thirteen years. When he closed his eyes he could still see all the empty corridors and locked doors in soft grey-scale tones. Sometimes he thought maybe they were just flickering photographs – still lives that would never change. But then she appeared in the middle of the night and he never thought that again.

It was the early hours of Boxing Day. Green Oaks Shopping Centre closed only on Christmas Day and Easter Sunday, and Kurt always worked both as part of the two-man skeleton crew. The customers didn't like it when the centre shut. On Christmas Day he'd seen the usual small angry crowd banging on the glass doors demanding admission. He watched them on the monitor and thought how like zombies they were. The undead demanding refunds and exchanges.

Now in the security office with only a beaten up Philips radio for company, he leaned back in the leather swivel chair and unscrewed the lid of his thermos – he wondered if it was too early to start his sandwiches. The DJ was dedicating 'Wichita Lineman' to Audrey in Great Barr. Kurt quietly sang along with Glen. Scott had drawn the short straw and was out in the darkness, patrolling the icy, still car parks around the perimeter. Kurt couldn't help but smile.

The camera view changed and twenty-four new flickering vistas opened up on screen. On the top left monitor he caught a brief glimpse of Scott walking diagonally across the bottom half of the screen. His breath was visible for a second before and after his image appeared.

Kurt had a new year's resolution. It was a week early, but he knew what it was already. It was easy to remember because it was the same as last year and the year before: he was going to quit his job and get out of Green Oaks. But this time he meant it. He'd never intended to stay in the job long and now thirteen years had passed and he didn't know where they'd gone. Patrolling empty corridors, eating sandwiches in the middle of the night, looking at his reflection in the one-way glass. He seemed incapable of leaving: something always held him back. It bothered him that life was slipping through his hands and all he seemed able to do was watch it go. He had no ambition to do anything else, but he thought that he should.

He closed his eyes and imagined a thermal image taken from high above – with him and Scott as two tiny red dots at the centre of a vast cold blue shadow covering the heart of the Midlands. In a few hours the centre would be packed with bodies and Scott and he would be lost amidst all the other blobs of colour swarming and merging. Kurt had volunteered for a double shift, but was dreading the noise and confusion of the day ahead. The other guards had families and liked to spend bank holidays with them. In particular they seemed to like spending those days with their families at Green Oaks or sometimes, for a change, another shopping centre further afield. Kurt would see them grimly pushing their way through the holiday crowds, trying to enjoy life on the other side. Free time – what were they supposed to do with it?

He bit into a fishpaste sandwich and looked at his watch: it was 4 a.m. Six till eight were the best hours of the shift for him. He loved to watch the first, tentative encroachments made by the early workers. He liked to see the cleaners implacably removing all trace of the day before, wiping away fingerprints, brushing up hair, hoovering dust, tampering with evidence. He felt his head being cleansed with every stroke. The screaming baby, the violent pensioner, the useless shoplifter, the desperate woman, the lonely man, the mysterious lift shitter . . . all deleted one by one. All sealed in bin bags and wheeled off down grey corridors to waiting waste containers. The centre waking up was like a lullaby to him, which soothed and calmed him before he went home to sleep.

As he reached for his crisps something caught the corner of his eye and he looked back at the wall of monitors. He saw the figure standing in front of the banks and building societies on level 2. It was a child, a girl, though her face was hard to see. She stood perfectly still, a notebook in her hand and a toy monkey sticking out of her bag. Kurt spun round to pick up his radio and signal Scott, and as he turned back to the screens he saw her disappear out of picture. He changed camera view: nothing. He rapidly clicked through each of the monitors' camera positions, but there was no sign of her. He was surprised to feel his tired heart beating hard as he called to Scott.

*

At 6.55 a.m. Lisa parked and took the lift from the frozen underground car park up to level 1 of Green Oaks Shopping Centre. She hated the trauma of her 5.30 a.m. alarm call, and she hated most of the seventeen waking hours that followed, but there was something soothing about the hushed predictability of the short walk across the mall early every morning. The indistinguishable chimes of muzak merged with the smell of cleaning chemicals and Lisa's own groggy weariness to create a floating, ethereal feeling.

The female voice of the lift requested that she wait for the doors to open. Lisa wasn't so impatient as to attempt anything else. A ping announced the parting of the doors and she stepped out into the artificial dawn of the central atrium. It was Boxing Day – guaranteed chaos – but all was peaceful at this hour.

She seemed to glide along the polished walkways, past the army of cleaners who tended, buffed and stroked the centre. Lisa thought 'cleaners' was too crude a description. At Green Oaks the generic process of cleaning was fractured into fifty or sixty different task groups, each one more esoteric than the last. None of the cleaners seemed to be of normal working age. It was as if a war had claimed all those between sixteen and sixty. Maybe not a war, just better-paid jobs. Either way, the sight of apparent children working alongside the limping, rheumatoid elderly gave Green Oaks a real workhouse authenticity.

Today she passed Ray first, one of the legion of window cleaners, pulling his squeegee across the glazed planes of Burger King. There was something about Ray that made you want to shout 'All right, Ray?' louder than was necessary each time you saw him, eliciting the never varying 'Lovely, ta'. A few yards from Ray was a young boy with a bottle of baby oil and a cloth, slowly shining the four miles of metal railings around the centre as he did every day. Up on the mezzanine she passed the skyjack, a motorized elevated cradle on wheels. In the cradle a young man thrust a synthetic duster into each of the millions of apertures in the plastic lattice ceiling grid above his head, before moving the vehicle on a few more feet.

But not everyone was visible. Lisa was keenly aware of the hidden security presence in the centre. Every morning she felt those tired eyes upon her and was hyper-conscious of her every movement. The constant weight of surveillance made her feel suspicious and, over time, this sense of guilt had developed into a little game she liked to play. She imagined that inside her bag, instead of an aged satsuma and seventeen empty envelopes, she carried something clandestine: a small timed device, a secret message, an illicit package – it didn't matter what. In her head various genres had been mixed up to create some incoherent spy/terrorist/resistance-fighter fantasy – it changed from day to day, but always with the hidden security guards cast as the Nazis.

She imagined how convincing and natural a portrayal of an early-morning shift manager she was delivering for the cameras. She looked every inch the downtrodden drudge. Who would suspect such a miserable creature? Yes, she had chosen the shabby trainers well. She walked purposefully but calmly past Dunkin Donuts and Celebrations Cards, and as she passed through the mirrored doors into the service corridors she imagined the crackle of radio static and slurps of tea in the security room. She was sure she was raising no suspicions amongst the pudgy-handed biscuit munchers.

Once through the doors she moved stealthily along the grey concrete walls. If she was caught here the mission would fail. She left no fingerprints as she opened every swing door with her back, she leapt across openings and she always stopped and listened for footsteps before turning a corner. The goal was to reach the back door of Your Music without being seen by anyone in the corridors. She took it more seriously than she would like to admit. The previous week she had been embarrassed to find that someone from Dolcis had been walking twenty feet behind her up the stairs and must have observed the whole sorry pantomime.

Today she saw a guard up ahead so she ducked back into an inglenook behind a ventilation pipe until he passed. As she emerged she saw some cloth poking from behind the pipe lower down. Normally she would have left it. Bits of cloth poking out from behind old pipes were rarely something she wanted to get involved with. But still in a vaguely clandestine frame of mind, she took a closer look. It was some sort of cuddly toy. Gradually she eased him out and admired him. He was about eight inches high, wearing a pin-stripe suit and spats. He had a look on his face that said business. He was a monkey. Lisa was amazed by her find. He was some remarkable, intact fragment from another world just dropped from the sky. She couldn't fathom how he got there. He was a little dusty, and had some grey paint on his back, but aside from that he seemed almost alarmingly fresh and vital. Yes, he was indeed a dapper fellow, a monkey who wouldn't show you up in public, a monkey you could take anywhere with you. Lisa dusted him off and then, by means of a previously entirely superfluous loop on her bag, slotted him into place at the side of her. She walked on to work, not caring who saw her.

Unidentified Security Guard
Upper North Mall

As your eyes move over the crowd they snag on certain people. Maybe a shiny-faced girl with gold gypsy earrings. Maybe an old lady in a dark wig. It's like spinning a radio dial and seeing where the needle rests.

These faces amongst faces – what are they doing at Green Oaks? The lonely man shopping for new shirts. The unhappy couple trying to get through a Sunday. The woman trying to get anyone's attention. Four hundred thousand different stories on a busy day, floating up in the air like foil balloons, sticking to the ceiling.

Green Oaks is more than bricks and mortar, I've always known that. The voices merge and give the place its own sound. No one notices it, but they all hear it; it's what brings them here – the low-level static hiss. If you could tune to the right frequency the individual voices would break through and then you'd hear them all. You'd hear what they were hoping to find at Green Oaks. You'd hear how Green Oaks could help them. I think Green Oaks can help everyone. I think it hears all the voices.

16

It was going to be a truly hellish day at Your Music: bank holidays were pure pain. The centre would be packed and the customers would display that special lethal holiday blend of frayed tempers and stupidity; angry with themselves for having nowhere better to go. To make matters immeasurably worse the store was expecting a visit from Gordon Turner, the regional manager – a prospect that always sent Crawford over the edge of sanity.

Lisa was assistant manager at the Your Music superstore, working directly for its manager, the gangly, cadaverous Dave Crawford, and in theory supervising directly each of the five floor managers. Crawford referred to her as 'duty manager' and in this unilateral change of job title, he somehow had also subtly changed her role to become the member of management expected to do the worst shifts. She saw the store early mornings, late nights, Sundays and bank holidays. This, it seemed, was her duty.

Crawford was usually a steady source of comedy to Lisa. She never ceased to marvel at the way in which he could sustain a level of rage for weeks that most people could manage only for minutes. She loved the way his language became more macho and violent the more effete the topic he was enraged about ('What cunt scuffed this fucking fascia?'). She gasped at his rejection of logic and rationality. But she enjoyed best his complete lack of self-awareness – the way he always wore jeans too tight for him and would shamelessly pluck them out of his arse as he spoke, walking as if he'd been on a horse for weeks. This, in particular, disgusted store security, who felt emasculated enough that they were working for a homosexual, without this constant suggestion of anal discomfort.

Visits were opportunities for senior management to justify their positions. This was their chance to prove that they could effortlessly perform a better job of running the store than the current management team. They would point out missed sales opportunities, sloppy merchandising, woeful lack of product knowledge, poor customer service, chewing gum on the carpet, overly pierced staff. Equally, if a member of staff screwed up, then Crawford would be seen to have screwed up, and if Crawford screwed up then Turner screwed up, and so the binding cement of anxiety, panic and blackmail was spread thickly from the sixteen-year-old Saturday girl up to the regional manager.

But at Green Oaks, unfortunately for Crawford, the Your Music staff no longer cared. They had been in a state of permanent high alert and blackmailed into unpaid overtime for the previous three months, as visit after visit had been announced and then suddenly cancelled at the last minute. Cancellations were part of the game: no harm shaking a store up a bit with the threat of a visit, no need really to carry out the threat. There had been sixteen cancelled visits in three months and, as the staff had grown more and more jaded and weary with visit fatigue, Crawford had grown increasingly manic and paranoid.

Lisa was waiting in Crawford's office, while he fussed about at the noticeboard, pinning up lots of graphs and tables with upward curves. She wasn't in the mood for him, she was too tired to be amused.

He finally finished set dressing and began speaking. 'Right, I had a walk around the store half an hour ago and it is a complete fucking shit-tip, it's a disaster. Have you seen the chart wall? There are three gaps in the Shakira display. I said to Karen, "What the fuck is that about?" and she goes, "Ooh, Dave, I ordered three hundred more on Monday. They're out of stock at the suppliers, we've got the last ninety-five in the region." Can you believe that? Can you believe the stupidity? I said to her, "If we've only got ninety-five what the fuck are they doing on the chart wall where customers can buy them? Take them off, put them behind the counter till we get the nod that Turner's on his way, then you can put them back out." She just looked at me, as if I was the one from another planet. Can you do something about her face? Can she look any more miserable? I feel like slashing my wrists every time I talk to her. If a mystery customer gets served by her we may as well close up and look for new jobs the same day.

'The next disaster area is the overstocks section in the stockroom. Have you seen it? Have you seen what's in it?'

Lisa realized with a start that this brief pause in the monologue was a cue for her to answer. She really didn't have the energy to be facetious, but after thinking and thinking of a possible alternative reply, she was forced to answer, 'Overstocks?'

'Exactly! Is it possible that everyone is so dim as to not realize that when we have a visit, the point of the overstocks section is not to store thousands of overstocks, like a big signed statement saying, "Yes, we are crap at buying, we make mistakes all the time." The point is for the overstocks section to be empty, for visitors to marvel at our precise stock control and turnover. Get Henry to fill some crates with the stock and take it and hide it in a cubicle in the ladies bogs.'

'There are only two cubicles, Dave, and one is already filled with boxes of Star Trek T-shirts.'

'Yes? And there are perfectly good public toilets out in the shopping centre. It's only for a day – or until they turn up anyway. That's exactly the kind of no-can-do attitude that is going to stop you from getting your own store.

'I've just had the same thing with that ape in security, whingeing on to me about fire exits being blocked with stock. He's wittering on about being the fire officer and loss of life. I can't believe someone that huge has no space for a brain. I spoke as slowly and loudly as I could, hoping it might reach him: I said, "Don't worry yourself. We will move the boxes before the next fire inspection. No one will know." Again that same look I see everywhere: he goes, "What if there's a fire today?" I just walked away. I can't deal with that kind of attitude.

'Then who should I see, or should I say sniff, in the corner of the stockroom, stickering stock, but little Pongo Snodgrass? I called across to him, "Oi, Graham, it's your lucky day, take the day off." So obviously all the other drones go quiet and start listening, they've no sensitivity. He said, "But there's loads of stock to process. I thought today was the visit." I said, "It is, but you've got the day off. Go and grab your coat." But no, still he doesn't get the message, and Henry's going to me, "It's all right, Dave, let me talk to him." And then Pongo pipes up again, "I don't understand why you want me to go home. It will just mean loads of work for the other lads. Henry asked if I'd work through my lunch hour cos I'm the fastest." What can I say? Everyone's looking at me, I have to be honest with him, so I say, "You might be the fastest, but you stink. You smell really, really awful. Everyone knows it, no one will say it, but I'm saying it cos I'm not having Gordon Turner gagging when he tours the stockroom. Go home and have a bath." You know I swear I saw that little ginger one go for me, but Henry held him back. They're a weird bunch up there, all inbred, I don't know how Henry manages them.

'So don't stand there gawping like a bloody guppy fish – go and sort it out.'

Lisa took the list she'd been making, left the stale tobacco fug of Crawford's office and went and opened the store.

*

Kurt and Gary each held onto an arm of the two youths as they pushed against the tides of shoppers towards the security suite. The boys had been on a spree, but they hadn't been very good. Their first mistake was dressing as if auditioning for roles as shoplifters in a TV drama. Kurt wished they would get over that. Scarves wrapped around faces, caps pulled down low, regular bandidos. It would make all their lives a lot simpler if they weren't so bloody awful at thieving. The boys strained half-heartedly against their captors while Radio Green Oaks played the Lighthouse Family. Shoppers looked on them with satisfaction, happy to know that no one was getting away with anything.

Kurt felt tired; the double shift was endless and he didn't think he had the stomach for Gary's forthcoming show trial. He couldn't imagine what it was about catching very stupid shoplifters that made Gary feel so clever. He knew the two boys would now be treated to a blow-by-blow account of each mistake they had made, and proudly shown the surveillance footage. Gary would keep saying 'Not so clever now, are you?' while he showed time and time again how he had outwitted them. Kurt had no interest in catching shoplifters. He thought maybe he was in the wrong line of work.

He sat in the corner and wondered where the girl was now. That night Scott and he had done a full search of the centre and the service corridors but had found no trace. They'd decided the most likely explanation was a runaway who'd concealed herself at closing time on Christmas Eve. Sometimes people wanted to escape from Christmas – sometimes they had no choice. Kurt had phoned the police, but no one had been reported missing yet. The policeman laughed and said this was the first time a kid had been found before it was lost. Kurt didn't see the joke. Something about the stillness of her had unnerved him. An image came into his head of the girl alone in the centre, singing: 'I once was lost, but now am found.'

Two hours left until he could go home. It was entirely likely that Gary's oration could last that long. The two felons were not reacting how Gary liked: they were neither crying at the prospect of parents and police being phoned, nor reluctantly according Gary respect for his crack surveillance. This wasn't what they'd come here for today. They'd probably come to pick up girls, and when that failed they thought they could pick up something else instead. They were playing with their zips and looking very bored. As bored as Kurt felt. This was bad. Gary's approach was attritional: he would continue until he got some satisfaction or the police turned up.

Kurt excused himself to write up the paperwork in the other room. Kurt didn't have a problem with paperwork. A lot of the guards despised it, thought it got in the way of the real job. Some of them would swear about it and get in a fury, then Kurt would offer to write it up for them, to save them the time, and no one would have to mention that they couldn't read or write. Kurt recognized the signs – the red-eared shame and embarrassment masked with a tabloid stared at avidly over lunch.

Scott was the only guard with whom Kurt felt comfortable. Scott had no shred of badness or bullshit in him. Scott had trusted Kurt with the secret of his illiteracy and asked Kurt to teach him to read and write. Kurt was amazed and proud at how fast Scott learned. The only downside of this arrangement was that Scott had become Jilly Cooper's unlikeliest fan. He had practised reading at home on whatever books his wife had lying around and now when he wasn't enthusing about West Bromwich Albion he'd be filling Kurt in on the latest naughtiness in the stables. He had recently started buying the *Daily Mail* each day, and Kurt wondered what monster he'd helped create.

Kurt finished his notes and looked out of the control room window – another pair of eyes scanning the mall. The ranks of centre security were augmented by the guards and store detectives most stores employed internally, amounting to around two hundred security officers working the four square kilometres of Green Oaks. Watchers, followers, waiters, suspicious minds, bored minds, looking for signs, looking for trouble. Kurt thought of those eyes, ringed with tiredness, darting about like flies. The security density at Green Oaks compared favourably with that in even the most turbulent parts of the outside world. Kurt wondered how much of the country had now been split off into these security fiefdoms. Patches of scorched earth almost bleached white by the constant surveillance of so many different eyes. He thought of his grandmother who had been badly beaten up in her own flat last year, and wondered when she might be considered as worthy of protection as a range of Nike baseball caps. He'd once made the mistake of mentioning this to Gary, who was an ex-copper, to which Gary replied, 'We don't need more police, just less niggers.'

Kurt's radio suddenly crackled and he put it to his ear to catch all the static.

17

Lisa sat in the window of Burger King consuming saturated fat and a large carton of sugar. It was a treat. She couldn't face the staff room. Turner had of course failed to turn up over Christmas again and now, only weeks later, Your Music had been tipped off to expect a visit from a mystery customer and Crawford was twitching. There was something in the air of Green Oaks that made everyone crave the complex non-flavours of highly processed, industrially honed calorific content – and Lisa was too tired to fight it today. Some of her colleagues at Your Music spent so much money on the stuff that she wondered if it wouldn't be easier for them to be paid with a weekly shot of modified starches and trans-fats straight into a prepared vein. She could quite easily imagine a group of industrially reared, drip-fed battery retail workers crammed behind a counter and Crawford rubbing his hands as his yield increased.

She watched the tail end of the January sales rush stream by on the other side of the glass. There were no external windows at Green Oaks and so it was only by looking at the shoppers that you could get some idea of the weather outside. Today everyone was dressed as American footballers – tight bundles of padding and head gear bouncing off each other. Some flushed faces had shed their layers and wadding and now looked like skinny new-born foals as they tripped lightly alongside the others.

Lisa watched a child trail behind its parents. The little

girl had a floppy fringe and something about her reminded her of Kate Meaney. Of course Kate wouldn't be a child now. She'd be an adult, just a couple of years younger than Lisa herself, but she found it impossible to think of her like that. The image in her head was always the same: a serious girl with sad blue eyes that followed you. Always watching.

Lisa had been twelve when Kate disappeared. The little girl who left her house one day and never came home – vanished into thin air. No witnesses, no sightings, no body. Lisa and Kate hadn't been friends; in fact they barely knew each other. Lisa had probably seen Kate three times in her life. But she remembered vividly the first time she'd met her.

Lisa had been standing outside her dad's sweet shop, bored of waiting for him. As she waited, she became aware of someone standing a little further along the road in another shop doorway, peeping out. Lisa leaned forward to get a better look and as she did so the figure pulled back. This sequence was repeated a few times until Lisa gave in and walked along to investigate. She found a little girl in baseball boots and a donkey jacket, standing with a notebook. When the girl saw Lisa she jumped and tried to put the notebook away.

'What you doing?' said Lisa.

'Nothing,' Kate replied.

'You're doing something. Are you spying on me? Are you drawing me? Cos if you are you have to give it to me cos I'm the sole owner of my image and you have no right to its reproduction and if you try and do that I can sue you for defamation and plagiarism and . . . copyright.'

Kate blinked and said in a small voice, 'I'm watching Mrs Leek's maisonette over the road. She's gone on holiday and I'm keeping an eye out for suspicious characters trying to case the joint.'

Lisa stared at Kate for a long time. Then she said, 'What?'

'Felons who want to gain access illegally and abscond with Mrs Leek's belongings.'

Lisa took a while to let this information sink in. 'How long have you been stood here with your notebook?'

'Not long. Maybe an hour and a half. Today, anyway.'

Lisa reeled at this. 'And what you got written down?'

Kate dutifully opened the book, which had various minutely scrawled thumb tabs along the side, and flicked to a particular section. She read the page carefully and then said, '16.03 – cat goes to toilet in front garden.'

'That's it?'

Kate studied the page again. 'So far, yes. A small boy passed by on a trike earlier but I ruled him out as a suspect. He's three.'

Lisa was trying to imagine standing in the same spot for an hour and a half, but she couldn't. She found ten minutes of stillness excruciating.

Kate cleared her throat and said, 'What do you do to your hair?'

Lisa's hand shot up to her head. 'What's the matter? Is it flat? Is it lop-sided? What's happened?'

'No, it's very standy-uppy. I just wondered how you did that. Do you have to sleep in a special way or eat special food?'

This was the kind of question Lisa dreamt of. 'Well, for this particular style you can't wash it too often or else you get that kind of fluffy Howard Jones look and everyone wants to kick you. Wash it every three or four days. After you've washed it, you put as much gel on as you can and then you blow-dry it upside down and rub the top of your head really hard the whole time – that way you get a classic "Mac" McCulloch look. Obviously if you wanted more of a Robert Smith you'd have to backcomb individual strands more. Don't use soap though – only old man punks use soap to make it stand up – you don't want to look like you're from the Exploited or something. Then spray it with hairspray, but not an expensive one. If you use something fancy like Elnette it's not gonna do the job. You need something cheap and sticky – Harmony is good. And remember that the rain is your enemy.'

Kate had listened very closely to this, and though she could understand many of the words used, the overall effect was entirely incomprehensible.

Lisa continued: 'Do you want me to do it to you? I could if you wanted.'

Kate thought about this for very little time. 'No thank you. It's important that I don't draw attention to myself. It's not appropriate in my line of work.'

Lisa was entirely puzzled by this response and was grateful to see her dad finally emerge from the shop. She ran off after him without another word to Kate.

She remembered driving off in the back of her dad's Datsun estate, looking over her shoulder and seeing Kate still standing there in the fading light, notebook in hand.

Now, leaving half of her burger uneaten, Lisa leaned against the glass balcony on level 4 and looked down on the heads of people on the ground floor. Around the edges, movement was quick and fluid: people disappearing into and emerging from the different outlets, stepping in and out of the liquid stream. Closer to the centre the pace was more sluggish: cruising groups of teenagers and older people with no purpose, just ambling along, taking it all in. They'd be the first people in, the last people out, the terminal moraine of the glacier. Lisa wondered if they ever left the centre. She imagined them rumbling around in the early hours, packed together in the darkened lanes. In the centre of all the movement a security guard stood immobile. He rolled his head back on his shoulders and stared at the glass ceiling high above him and Lisa stared down into his sad face. Their eyes connected for a minute and Lisa felt a little dizzy leaning over the balcony. She realized she should get back to the shop.

Green Oaks was not a pleasant place to work. In 1997 the management team of the centre, in accordance with the strategic business objectives of Leisure Land Global Investments (owners of forty-two retail parks around the world), sent out their first annual questionnaire to ascertain working conditions for the nine thousand staff at the centre. It revealed levels of dissatisfaction so consistent and so acute that, unknown to its subjects, it later went on to become a case study for undergraduate sociologists. A second survey never materialized.

The key problem with Green Oaks was the gulf between conditions for customers and conditions for staff. The centre was built at a time when the idea of turning a shopping centre into some larger leisure experience was just beginning to gain currency in Europe. The architects and planners of the Mark 2 Green Oaks embraced the idea of creating an unparalleled experience for shoppers – with verdant rest areas, ergonomic seating, light and airy atriums, water features, convenient parking, vast and lavish public toilets. In contrast, staff areas in each store were cramped to allow maximum sales floor footage. Staff facilities were of an extremely low level: few toilets, dark interior areas, outdated and ineffective ventilation and heating, bare breeze-block walls, constant sewage odours and significant rat infestation. The staff felt this apartheid keenly. They read the memos from management requesting that they did not use customer toilets and rest areas, they watched as their car parking area was moved further and further away from the centre, they passed every day from the light-filled atriums to the gloomy service corridors:

long, grey tunnels which Lisa used now to reach the back door of her store.

Your Music had five sales floors, and above them a sixth floor for the stockroom and staff room. She tried to pass quickly through the stockroom. This area was staffed by two types of people: those lacking the basic skills or hygiene to make it onto the shop floor, and those who had taken all they could of customers and would now rather sticker stock all day than trust themselves near members of the public. None of the latter group, which included Henry, the efficient but depressed stockroom controller, was in today. Instead there were four seventeen-year-olds. Three Matts and a Kieron. They all had the same straggly long hair, they all earnestly nodded their heads to extremely loud nu-metal all day long, and they all managed to fuck up even the simplest of instructions all the time. Lisa waited for the lift and tried not to think about the fleeting glimpses of chaos she had seen. Five minutes later she was still waiting, trying not to react to the loud crashes and occasional yelps from behind her.

Customers had a choice and could move between floors of the store either by the wide gentle stairways, or by the cramped lift. The vast majority, still enchanted by its early 1980s glass sides, eagerly chose the lift. Staff had no such choice: typing a special key code into the lift was the only way to get themselves and stock to and from the sixth floor. The lift was a constant source of distress for them, as customers' floor requests were programmed to override the staff key code, and it could often take several teeth-grinding journeys up and down the liftshaft before it would finally take them to the sixth floor. Inevitably a few confused customers would always be carried up in the lift when it finally made its ascent. Usually they would gasp or scream in horror as the lift door opened to reveal that they had somehow been taken off-map to somewhere they should not be. Occasionally, however, one would disembark, oblivious to the breeze-block walls, cardboard boxes, shrinkwrap machines and lack of all shop-floor signifiers. They would make their way through the stockroom, absently looking about them for *Touch of Frost* videos, and become aggressive when staff attempted to herd them back into the lift.

Every now and then, perhaps bristling at the unwavering flow of hatred directed at it, the lift would suddenly disregard all floor requests and plunge at high speed down below the ground floor into an unused subterranean extension of the shaft, where it would sulk in its hole for anything from thirty seconds to, on one occasion, two hours (inevitably, in that instance containing Unlucky Kieron from the stockroom). Most staff had experienced this petulance at some point and, as the lift had started its swift descent, all without exception had been momentarily convinced that the cable had snapped and they were racing towards a concertinaed end. But what of those times it happened to customers? Who could imagine what went on in their minds? It was a rare but always special moment to be standing behind the counter on the ground floor and see the lift shoot past, the figures pressed against the glass a caricature of eye-bulging, arm-waving alarm. Today, as the lift arrived, Lisa was massively relieved to find it empty.

*

Kurt was slowly patrolling through the parallel unseen universe of the service corridors. Mile upon mile of pipes, wires, ventilator shafts, fuse cupboards, security barriers, fire hoses. Like an illuminated cave network, narrow passages would abruptly bloom into cavernous loading bays and other lanes would lead nowhere. Everything glowed grey, everything smelled of hot dust. He would wander for hours in a trance, following no particular route, going through the motions of checking every door handle. Sometimes he'd stop and try and sense where he was in relation to the centre, but he rarely came close. He liked to be lost, tangled somewhere in the knotted orbit of the mall.

It was here in the corridors that he could delicately finger the familiar edges of the textures in his head. Many of his memories of Nancy were fading and he didn't know if this was good or bad. He was glad some of the pain was fading, had already faded so much since the first year. But it seemed to be a trade off: with the pain went details and memories. People had said, 'Time heals,' but he realized time didn't heal, time just eroded and confused, and he didn't think that was the same thing at all. It was four years since she had been killed. Sometimes when he was at home in the afternoon, the sun would shine in a certain way through his bedroom window, the net curtain would move in the breeze, causing a rippling shadow on the wall, and he'd have a strong sense-memory of what it felt like to be loved, what it felt like to fall asleep and wake up with someone's hand in yours. He'd try and hold onto this sensation of euphoria as long as he could but it was only ever momentary. Mainly, all he could dredge up of certain times were memories of memories. He was scared to think back too much, frightened that repeated playing would wear the memories out completely. He'd already forgotten how she laughed. He felt the weight and responsibility of being the only person guarding all these memories. It made him panic sometimes, as if he was trying to hold water in his hands. He wanted to download the memories somewhere safe, keep them backed up. The only thing that made her real was the boxes and boxes of her stuff that crowded his flat. But the boxes didn't make him feel good; they just added anxiety to his grief. There was so much crap in them, he was scared to open them. For every significant letter there were ten curled bank statements. One box was filled with the junk mail that still kept coming for her – so many once-in-a-lifetime opportunities that she'd missed by dying. Kurt curated the collection, though he didn't know who for.

He patrolled on. Many of the security guards thought that stretches of the corridors were haunted. They heard banging on doors or whispers on empty stairwells, felt sudden temperature drops, found hoses unravelled. Kurt listened to them in coffee breaks, like old women trying to outdo each other. No-shit tales full of shit. Earnest head-nodding, comically superstitious. Kurt felt no trace of the paranormal as he drifted through the passageways, but sometimes a certain uneasiness would fill him. Occasionally he'd turn a corner and find himself in a cul-de-sac – a service passageway that had nowhere to go, nothing to service – and there was something about the blank brick wall ahead that made his stomach shrink as he remembered the old house he'd grown up in and the nightmares he'd had as a child. For a moment he'd be scared to turn around, feeling that someone had been following him to this full stop. He would back away rather than turn his back on the wall, but still a feeling of being watched remained. He felt it in the buzzing in his ears, the pressure behind his eyelids. 'Anyone there?' he'd say, and always wish he hadn't.

Tonight he thought about the little girl he'd seen on the monitor weeks earlier. He'd rung the police again, but still no report of a missing child. He couldn't shake the feeling that she was somewhere in the passages with him. He wished he could find her and return her home.

Kurt felt tired. He could easily just sit down on the concrete floor and nod off, but that would be a bad idea. He had started sleeping a lot after Nancy died. He had got to a stage where he could sleep as much as he wanted. The problem had been deciding how much that was. In the first year he would sleep whenever he wasn't working or eating. He could sleep through a night, and if the following day was his day off, he could catnap through that too.

He'd not been too bothered by the realization one day that sleep had become an addiction. But he started to find it hard to distinguish between dreams, reality and memory. He became scared that sleep was making him forget the true Nancy. Dreams could trick him: they would pose as memories, pretend to have a history; they would contain other dreams. He realized too late that dreams were a creeping encephalitic virus that he had allowed to colonize his mind, and now it was spreading and linking and eating the truth – deleting the facts. Already large parts had gone. Had he and Nancy once sat in a crowded bar and unsuccessfully tried not to watch a couple making love in the corner? Had they once seen a huge chunk of ice glistening on the forest floor on a sunny day? Had he really been having the same recurring dream of Nancy in a red hat since he had known her? Or had he dreamt that last night for the first time, and with it dreamt of the recurrence? He was appalled that he had no answers to these questions and so, after a year of somnolence, he went to see the doctor. The doctor referred him to specialists and Kurt spent several nights in a sleep clinic. In the end they told him lots of things his condition wasn't. It wasn't narcolepsy – though he had symptoms of hypnagogic hallucinations. It wasn't apnea – his breathing was fine. At a loss, they finally said it was idiopathic hypersomnia. One consultant told Kurt that this was a scientific way of saying 'we don't know'. They had eliminated all other possibilities; it was 'a diagnosis of exclusion'. The exclusion part Kurt understood. The doctor told him to stop shift work, which he couldn't, and strictly limit himself to eight hours' sleep a night, which he could, eventually.

It had been hard for many months. Sleep would curl slowly around him while he was reading a book, sleep would trick him that he was awake, sleep would play the best movies. Gradually, though, he fought through it and, as with any addict, he found life now stretched second by second, and even four years on he would sometimes feel sleep offering its old answer.

At night in the passageways he would remember Nancy and it would seem like imagination, and sometimes he would imagine the lives of the people in the shopping centre and it would seem like memory. He tried hard to get the distinction right, but some bad osmosis was messing it all up.

Anonymous Male
East Upper Mall

I'll just pop into Your Music and have a look in the video section. There's no harm in that. A quick look in the section as I'm passing, but I won't enquire at the counter. I'm passing anyway. It's on my way. I don't have anything special to do today, so I can buy a newspaper at WHSmith and if I'm there I may as well pop in.

I could buy the newspaper at the shop next door to me, and then I suppose I'd save the bus fare, but I never know what paper I want till I get in there, and Smiths has a fantastic selection. It will probably be the Mirror, *but at least I have the choice. And I have to try and break the routine. That's what the lady at the clinic said last time. She said, 'Surprise yourself some days, break the pattern.' So maybe I'll do that today. Maybe today I'll buy the* Daily Gleaner *or the* Morning Star *or the London* Times *or the Manchester* Guardian. *The lady said I shouldn't come in here any more, but I think it's OK if I'm passing anyway. I think she'd say it's fine to have a quick, passing glance at the section if I'm on my way through to buy a newspaper . . . who knows which one.*

Oh, I thought that was a new video there, but I see it's just they've moved the section around, or maybe someone else picked up that episode and put it back in the wrong place. It made me stop, though, because I know the top left spine is always yellow for series 4, but that was orange, which is series 3. I've had to stop now. I wouldn't have stopped otherwise, but it was out of order, so I may as well help them out and put it back where it should be. I thought it was a new video, a new release. But I know they said there weren't any more. They said that last time. They said there was no point me checking every day, there were no more episodes to be released. Anyway I won't check at the counter, I won't ask if something has come out, cos they said last time nothing would.

It's just as well I'm not going to enquire because it's the girl with red hair behind the counter today. I heard her last time, she sighed. She was rude to me. She has no right to be rude to me, I'm a customer, and I'm allowed to ask about new releases. She was rude to me. She didn't say anything, but it was the way she looked, and when I heard her sigh, I knew it. Well, I'm not going to ask her today. She might see me over here and expect me to go up and ask her but I'll show her that she doesn't know me at all, that that isn't what I do any more. I'm off to buy a newspaper. I don't know which one yet. I'll buy the newspaper, then maybe I'll pass back through here on the way back to the bus stop. She might be on her lunch. I might get the lad with the spastic legs; he's never rude. I think he knows more about it than she does anyway.

18

When Kurt was eleven he used to have the house to himself on Friday nights. His parents would go out to the club, his older sister stopped over at her best friend's – and he would stay in and eat all the crisps and chocolate he could stomach. He'd lie along the sofa, trainers still on, illicitly balancing a glass of coke on the Dralon arm, and watch *The Professionals*. But over the sound of the telly he would hear other sounds – the clock ticking, the fridge buzzing, the stairs cracking explosively – and he felt very sure that the house was watching him. He would walk from room to room, turning lights on, sometimes shouting out, but the hostility remained. He'd retreat to bed and lie drifting in and out of sleep, waiting to hear his father's key turn in the lock, and he knew he was being watched even beneath the duvet. He felt the implacable presence pressing down on him.

The next morning he'd tell his mom how Bodie had totalled another car, and he'd recreate a few of Doyle's moves on the kitchen lino, and he wouldn't mention anything about the house and the noises and his fear. The next Friday it would happen all over again.

When he was twelve his family moved to a new house and it all stopped, but sometimes now in the dead slow hours between three and five, as he sat alone in the security office, he would hear a noise behind him or he would smell Nancy clearly in the room with him and that old sensation of tightness would return.

Kurt ate his sardine and tomato-paste sandwiches and looked at his reflection in the darkened glass of the office. He wondered if his appearance had changed much since Nancy's death: his hair was still the same, a bit greyer maybe; he still looked worried, perhaps more so now. He looked at his shoes and wondered if she'd have liked them. You could never tell. Often the line dividing something that Nancy loved and something she hated was invisible to him. He'd tentatively pick up a jumper in a shop and she would recoil and hiss, 'Look at the seams!' Nancy said Kurt had no awareness of subtlety. Kurt said that Nancy was insane, always citing some ridiculously esoteric objection. She once returned a blouse he'd bought her because she thought the buttonholes were at the wrong angle.

Kurt suspected he might have made some error in purchasing his current shoes – he wasn't sure about the placing of the eyelets. He had no trust in his own judgement any more, but there was no one else to rely on.

*

As Lisa reached the shop floor she noticed that there were now twelve units across the store dominated by Queen's *Greatest Hits* Volumes 1 and 2. This morning there had been four, which she had thought was overkill, but in a brief but colourful exchange with Crawford, a difference of opinion on this matter became clear.

She finally got to the counter just five minutes late to cover Dan's lunch. Her first customer was a middle-aged woman with eyebrows drawn on very high up her forehead.

'Save me looking, love,' said the lady. 'Where's that Queen one?'

As Lisa led the customer back to one of the eight Queen display units she had passed on her way to the counter, it occurred to her that the woman might be blind, and this would shed light on the misplaced eyebrows as well. She sometimes wondered if some people would rather be blind. 'Save me looking' was something she heard several times a day, and she couldn't understand what the big effort was in visual reception. She was unsure if it was acute laziness that led someone to ask someone else to use their eyes for them, or some belief that vision was a finite resource that they didn't want to wear out.

The rest of the hour was the usual Saturday afternoon blur of till activity. The TV ad campaign for Queen was working its dark magic and every other customer was clutching a copy of the *Greatest Hits*. In each of these households last night someone had seen a fresh promotional advert for an album that had been around for years and now they had to have it. It frightened her to witness these mass ebbs and flows, to work at the cutting face of all that suggestion and manipulation.

With one part of Lisa's mind switched to auto-pilot serving customers, the other part was free to wander as it always did. She'd been thinking about her brother a lot recently – maybe it was the impending twentieth anniversary, maybe it was just the natural cycle of memory. She tried to conjure up his face somewhere in the mass of customers around her, but found it hard to remember his features and it was impossible to imagine what he might look like now.

Most people think that it's a rare and difficult thing for a person to vanish completely. They believe that everyone turns up again eventually – alive or dead, religiously or chemically altered. But Lisa had seen it happen twice in her life. First Kate Meaney and then, not long after, her own brother.

Vanishing didn't seem like a freak occurrence to Lisa: the sudden removal of someone from your life was always a possibility. If her boyfriend Ed was late back from a club she'd wonder if he'd gone for ever – fallen between the cracks never to return. The horrible thing with Ed was that she wasn't sure that she'd really notice; most days she barely seemed to register his presence. Her brother's absence, though, was vast and unbearable. It felt as if a side of her self had fallen away, leaving her exposed. She reacted like her father, by crawling and hiding in a corner of life. They kept themselves busy and tried not to think about Adrian. Lisa dragged herself to school each day, did the homework they gave her, spoke in French when asked to, sat by herself on the bus. Her father served customers, drove to the wholesalers, counted piles of coins on the kitchen table and opened boxes of crisps. Her mother, on the other hand, was born again and devoted herself to Jesus and the unreliable-looking minister at the local Pentecostal church.

Lisa knew now that disappearing wasn't so rare. Ten thousand people managed it every year. Her brother was buried far down on the National Missing Persons Helpline website – an old photograph of him hidden under many, many photos of more recent mysteries. Scanning back through the pages, she could watch the hairstyles and collar sizes change. Lisa imagined the images scrolling back endlessly past whey-faced Victorian children and Civil War deserters. Inscrutable portraits with dead eyes. Adrian's photo was on the same page as Kate Meaney's. Every year on her birthday Lisa got a compilation tape from her brother. No letter, no address, no – as far as she could discern – hidden message in the choice of songs. The only message was that he was alive.

Some people – including the police – had believed Lisa's brother was responsible for Kate Meaney's disappearance. It was a belief that her brother couldn't live with and it had driven him to vanish. But Lisa never doubted him.

Although Lisa had only met her a few times, Kate Meaney had virtually lived in her father's shop. Kate had got on well with Adrian. They spent time together. Lisa had never thought it strange that a man of twenty-two should have a friendship with a girl of ten. She never thought it strange that he chose to work in a sweetshop rather than do something with his degree. Perhaps her dad thought differently – but Lisa never thought her brother was odd.

On 7th December 1984 Adrian was seen catching a bus with Kate Meaney from Bull Street in Birmingham city centre. Kate was never seen again. Various witnesses saw them on the bus together. One remembered the girl being reluctant to get off the bus and the man dragging her by the arm roughly. When questioned, Adrian said he had agreed to accompany Kate to the entrance examination for prestigious boarding school Redspoon. He said that Kate didn't want to take the exam and he had gone to lend moral support. He said that she'd been insistent that he didn't wait for her, which he didn't, but he took her as far as the gates and watched her walk up the drive and into the school. His story was contradicted, however, by the fact that Kate never arrived at Redspoon that day and no paper was ever received from her.

Lisa had heard the facts many times. She'd read horrible things in the newspapers. She'd seen the graffiti on their house. None of it impinged on her. Facts were irrelevant when you had true faith. She never once doubted her brother. She tried to imagine what really happened to Kate: who had come and snatched her from that school. She tried to conjure up a malevolent janitor, a homicidal groundsman – and if none of these scenarios quite rang true, she still never suspected her brother.

Lisa drifted back to the present as she noticed a middle-aged man seemingly lost in the middle of the floor. There was too much of a queue to leave the counter, so she could do nothing but watch his paralysis as hordes of shoppers moved past him. She saw a boy with a spiv moustache deliberately bang into the man and then curse him for standing in the way. Freddie Mercury was assuring everyone that they were the champions. Lisa and the lost guy knew differently.

19

Kurt Sr had high expectations of his children's conduct. Kurt and his sister were seen as models of good behaviour by every parent on the estate: polite, quiet, clean. Kurt Sr was a taciturn man who, like almost every other man on the estate, had lost his job when the economy changed. First the gas works closed, then the coking plant, then the factories, including the massive machine-tool manufacturing plant where Kurt Sr worked. Unlike most, however, Kurt Sr had managed to find another job in manufacturing – a real job, he would say. He got up at 4.30 every morning and sat on a bus for two hours to reach a factory on the outskirts of Birmingham. He seemed an old-fashioned man: he worked hard; he was courteous to women; he expected children to respect their elders; he was never seen shopping with his wife.

Kurt's mother, Pat, though naturally inclined to be softer than his father, deferred to her husband in everything. Every request was inevitably greeted with: 'You'll have to ask your father.' Kurt Sr decided everything, and once decided, nothing was questioned. The family feared him. He had a passion for Country and Western and yet treated this with the same dour gravitas he did every other aspect of his life. Every Friday night he took his wife to the local working men's club, where everybody dressed up in country gear and danced to Jim Reeves and Patsy Cline. Kurt Sr saw no frivolity in dressing up, and would solemnly press his black western shirt, and polish the metal discs on his black ten-gallon hat before leaving the house. At the club he would dance stiffly but accurately to the 'Tennessee Waltz' and other mid-tempo numbers, and he would always dance with the widow Mrs Gleason for one song, because he was a gentleman.

Being the child of the man was a heavy burden to carry and both Kurt and his sister buckled under the weight. His sister chose the more spectacular path, but for Kurt, rebellion was the small personal freedom of truancy. In the year around his tenth birthday he took occasional days off school. His parents never knew; he doctored sick notes and kept the truancy to an inconspicuous level.

Days away from school were days away from the expectations everyone had of him and the only opportunity he ever had to be his own person, out from under the shadow. He didn't do it against his father, but for himself: it felt essential, even though the thought of his father finding out made him sick with shame. Then one day he had a close shave – he couldn't remember now what it was – some badness that meant he had almost been caught, and it scared him into stopping.

Before then, Kurt had spent his truant days wandering through the silent remnants of industry that surrounded his estate: the gas holders of the old gas works, the cooling towers, the empty factories, the strange-coloured pools, the black brick huts, the canal, the embankment without a railway line. Some of the factories were demolished, some only half so; the cooling towers, too dangerous to blow up, were waiting to be dismantled brick by brick. These were the places where Kurt's father and the other men from the estate had grown up and worked; their absence imbued the landscape with a melancholy that Kurt was drawn to. He would wander through the slow, silent afternoons never seeing anyone else among the weeds and the bricks. He would climb through a window or a hole in a wall and find another vast cement plateau littered with rusting metal offcuts, and mysterious extruded shapes that he'd cram in his pockets. He revelled in the spaces, made dens in their corners and angles. He loved the sound metal coils of wire would make when the wind blew over them, loved the way the air smelled of ammonia, loved how he felt he was the last person alive on earth, shouting strange words at the peeling walls. Sometimes he might have to throw stones at a mean-looking dog, but that was all.

In the yard of one old factory on Long Acre there was a square hole in the concreted ground; a rusted metal ladder fixed to the side of the hole led down to darkness. Kurt spent a lot of time looking into the hole, wanting to descend but needing to see that nothing bad was down there first. He'd lie on the ground above the hole and peer into the blackness, waiting for shapes to emerge. Sometimes a shift in the sun would send light further down the shaft, but he could never see where the ladder ended. He wondered if it was a bomb shelter, or somewhere to store dangerous chemicals, or the place where lazy workers were sent. He wondered if there was treasure down there.

One day he took his father's torch from its place under the kitchen sink. He shone the torch down the hole, but still couldn't see how far the chamber extended. He lowered himself slowly down the ladder, but as he realized how far it stretched he started to panic about descending into the darkness without the use of his arms or the torch so he scrambled down more quickly, almost slipping off the rungs. It came as a jarring shock when he finally reached the bottom. He shone the torch around and saw that the space was as big as a classroom. The room smelled damp and cold. Bits of paper littered the floor. Kurt picked up a couple and shone his torch on them. They were old manuals: technical drawings and equations on yellowed brittle paper. There was no coherence to the items scattered across the room: an old scrolling blackboard with nothing written on it, bits of machinery, a broken umbrella. He walked slowly to the furthest end of the space. There were no beer cans or other signs of recent habitation. Kurt was sure he had discovered the ruin – the first explorer to come across this fallen empire. As he reached the far corner he turned round to look towards the entrance and was frightened to see that his torch beam didn't extend that far. All he could see was the abandoned chamber with no way out. He was suddenly overwhelmed with one thought: no one in the world knew where he was at that moment. He was entirely hidden, vanished from the earth. The realization was suffocating and unbearable, and as it expanded to fill his mind the old battery in the torch gave up and died. Blackness surrounded him and for a moment he thought he was dead. He fled blindly. After a few seconds of scrambling he reached the ladder and grazed his knee as he raced back up, all the time terrified some malevolent force was going to pull his legs back down.

After that he thought of the hole as death – a place you could go and see what death was. He covered over the opening with a stray bit of hardboard and put stones on top. When he walked across that bit of ground he knew exactly what lay beneath his feet.

Kurt realised that his secret places and all his silent industrial playgrounds were going. He had watched the scaffolding go up, and now come down again, for the new shopping centre opening a few hundred yards away. Already his father had forbidden any of the family to visit Green Oaks. The shopping centre was built on the site of his old factory, and Kurt Sr clearly saw it as an insult to the whole area, a place where women would work and women would shop and nothing would be made of any value. Kurt, though, was curious to see inside. He wanted to see if the ghosts could survive.

*

Dan burst into the staff room.

'Fucking *hell*. It took ten fucking minutes to get down in the fucking lift because the fucking chimpy customers pressed every button and then cooed like imbeciles every time the lift stopped and – hey – wonder of wonders the doors opened on yet another – yes, you guessed it – floor of the fucking shop they were in. You'd think the doors were opening onto views from the Hubble telescope.

'"Where are we?" "Is this the games floor?" "I don't know. It says four." "What's four?"

'Jesus Christ! How do these people get out of their front doors? Then I finally reach ground floor, fight through the sea of flailing puffins milling about in the racks, leg it to Marks & Spencers, only to get stuck in the queue of that freaky woman with the waxy fingers. You know I timed her and it actually takes her forty seconds to peel apart each bag and get the sandwich in. It's un-fucking-believable. I thought I was going to have a heart attack I was getting so stressed. Why do they put her on the tills? She can't do the one thing in life she has to: put triangular plastic boxes into square polythene bags. They should give her rubber gloves – or better still chop her hands off, cos they do her no fucking good. So you know – aeons of eye-watering fumbling later I get my sandwich. Finally get back to work, endure lift-hell again and now I have precisely twenty minutes of my lunch *hour* left and I swear to God that if there's no milk in the fridge I'm going to saw my cock off with a rusty spoon.'

'There's no milk,' Lisa volunteered impassively.

Dan blinked, then sighed and slumped into the chair opposite, where he rested his head on the table.

The staff room stank of the overflowing bin in the corner. Kentucky Fried detritus lay on the floor, waiting for a cleaner to bend down and deal with it. 'What d'you get for lunch?' she asked.

Dan answered without lifting his head. 'Pesto and Parmesan kettle chips, brie and grape sandwich, "big, thick and smooth" er . . . smoothie and a profiterole dessert in a pot.'

'Jesus. Are you Caligula?'

Dan lifted his head and looked around him. 'Yeah, that's right, Caligula in all his splendour, enjoying the sweet scent of rotting fast food. I apologize for my opulence. I understand that working here, particularly on a Saturday, is to experience such unrelenting joy that one must mitigate it by eating – what is it today?' Dan surveyed Lisa's grey home-made sandwich. 'Oh, good God. Oh God, no – fishpaste? Are you real? The war's over, you know, rationing's ended. Why don't you fuck off to the office anyway? I thought that was where managers were supposed to take their three-hour lunches.'

Lisa smiled. 'You know I'm a double agent. I like slumming it with the kids then going back and reporting to senior management on the mutinous mutterings. That's how I got the great job I now have, by constantly selling out the dissidents and refuseniks.'

'Shit,' said Dan, as if in revelation.

'How has your day been anyway?' asked Lisa.

'The usual. Another opportunity to see humankind at its best. Some days I long for just the standard loonies – you know, a good solid Obsessive Compulsive worrying about lost episodes of *On the Buses*. It's the sane ones you have to watch the most. I've had approximately 417 customers complain that the CD they want was cheaper last week. So I've explained that's because the sale ended on Thursday, and they have without exception just looked at me and blinked and said, "But I want to buy it now," and I've said as politely as I can, "Well, I'm afraid it's full price now. Maybe you should have bought it on Thursday, when the store was festooned with fifteen by fifteen foot banners declaring "Last day for sale prices today". And then – this is the bit that gets me – they say, "That's against the law."

'What is that? Where do they get this legal shit from? Some crazy, scrambled idea of the law patched together from episodes of *Watchdog* and backs of cornflake boxes. They shouldn't be out on their own. The great thing, though, the thing that keeps me serene, is that they are too stupid to realize that there are in fact only eight days a year when we don't have a sale on, there's another one starting tomorrow. I stand there listening to their shit and it doesn't touch me because I know we've got fifteen hundred of that very CD upstairs waiting to be re-stickered with the new sale graphics and then it'll be back on the shop floor at its usual low price. Something that perhaps in the old days I might have told them, but not now, oh no –'

'That's quite a victory,' Lisa said, but Dan ignored her interruption.

'And then, this woman in a nice dress came up to the counter and asked me something. And I don't know why, but there was something about her that made me well disposed to her from the start. She had a nice, uncomplicated face, you know, she didn't look like she had a grievance or a complaint. So anyway she asks me this thing, but I couldn't understand the words. It was just noise that came out. I don't know if she'd recently left the dentist, or she was deaf, or she had a speech problem or what . . . but you know, whatever, it doesn't matter to me, I was happy to help anybody who wasn't hassling me about the sale. So I ask her to repeat it maybe two or three times, and it's getting really embarrassing cos I kind of get the odd word, but it makes no sense. So I keep apologizing, and finally I think, should I get a pen and paper?

Will that anger her? Is that insulting or insensitive or something? But it's getting desperate and a queue is forming, so I pass over a pen and paper, and her whole face lights up as if to say, "Excellent, why didn't I think of that?" So she starts to write her request down, and I'm feeling quite pleased with myself, and thinking how there still are nice people in the world who are worth helping and giving your time to, and she hands me back the piece of paper with a smile, and I smile at her too and look at it and it says: "Horror look no flim in video".'

'What?' asked Lisa.

'Exactly. "Horror look no flim in video". Which is actually what it sounded like she was saying. And she's looking at me with this expectant look on her face, nodding her head as if to say, "Now do you see?"'

'What did you do?'

'I just kind of nodded my head in a way that I hoped conveyed complete comprehension and control of the situation, then I told her she needed to go to the fifth floor and ask for Mike.'

Anonymous Youth
Upper Mall Sector 3

Three o'clock now. Three. We're leaning over the balcony on the upper level. There's some girls down below us by Baskin-Robbins. Four girls. One's got hair like Britney had two years ago. She's got a scarf that is not really Burberry covering half her face, but you can still see she's pretty. She's holding the mobile phone down in front of her and the other three are crowded round and laughing. She's got some nasty text. She's pretending to be shocked, but she keeps laughing too. She is very pretty even though I can only see her eyes, just like the ninja Pakis. Todd will want her, and in a minute he'll say that, and then he'll say

Keown can have the dark one, Gary can have the tall one, and he'll look at me and say he doesn't fancy mine much, and I won't either cos I can see all of her face and she is not pretty. She should wear the scarf. Now we're standing across the aisle from them and they've seen us. Todd is pretend fighting with Keown and he is saying fuck off and calling Keown a wanker and a cunt a lot louder than he usually does. I am watching the non-pretty one without the non-Burberry scarf. She is looking down the mall towards the exit. She is not laughing at Todd and Keown like the other girls. I would like to have the other girls more, but even though she is not pretty and she has no tits I would still have her. I want to sit in the park at night away from Todd and Keown and Gary. I want to sit on the bench by the pond, and you'd only know I'm there because you could see the orange tip of my menthol cigarette. It would be cold on the bench, but I would have a girl next to me. She would also be next to me on the bus, at the back upstairs. I would write her name on the seat and I would write my name next to it. I would buy her an eternity ring. I would tell my dad to fuck off. I would buy her songs that I knew she liked. I would tell Todd to fuck off. Now Todd is giving the pretty girl a cigarette, and Keown and Gary are edging over to the other two, and my girl is walking away without looking back.

20

Lisa had known many alarm clocks, and she knew that they were not in this world to be liked. Alarm clocks knew the deal: a good day started with being told to fuck off, a bad day started with being hurled across the room and having your guts spilled on the floor. She was amused by the futile attempts at self-preservation made by many alarm clocks: adopting the guise of beloved cartoon characters or a favourite football team – futile because even a sweet child would rather crush Snoopy's head to a wiry pulp than endure the awful noise. Lisa had spent a lot of her life shopping for alarm clocks. She found she got through clocks and toothpaste at about the same rate. The high turnover was due to two factors: first, the natural wastage of any alarm clock: smashed against walls, thrown out of windows, unsuccessfully flushed down the toilet; secondly, the user developing a natural resistance to the tone and pitch of the alarm itself, rendering it useless. And so each alarm clock she bought was obliged to be both more physically robust and more sonically repellent than the last. Her current choice, she would grudgingly admit, was a particularly successful model, now into the seventh month of its reign of terror. She had gone wrong in the past by assuming a correlation between price and effectiveness. She had wasted a lot of money with Braun, and with a Swiss mail order company. The current model had cost £1.49. It was essentially a digital watch face in a lightweight plastic sphere – too light really to get up any velocity when thrown across the room. The alarm was astonishing. It was made up not of bleeps or a bell, but rather a loud steady droning buzz. The sound induced the same kind of all-over body panic and meltdown that Lisa would feel just before she vomited. She could tolerate it for 1.5 seconds tops.

Today was a day off, and perhaps the single best thing about a day off was going forty-eight hours without the emetic buzz of the alarm. Sunlight was covering the bed and Lisa was dreaming about shooting a dog she'd once had, while her brother threw bones over the fence. The gunfire seemed to get louder and she woke up to hear a German voice screaming: 'Gott im Himmel, arrrrrrghghghgh!' She walked into the lounge where Ed was sprawled on the floor playing *Medal of Honour* with the volume up high.

Lisa lived with Ed and often wondered exactly how this had come to pass. Naturally, Ed worked at Your Music – Lisa didn't meet any other types of people. They had fallen into some kind of a relationship about a year ago and now neither seemed to have the energy or impetus to leave. She was too tired usually to think about it, and when she wasn't too tired, she found other excuses. Despite working together, different shift patterns and areas of responsibility meant Ed and Lisa seldom crossed paths at the shop and at home there weren't too many occasions when they were both awake at the same time. Lisa thought she should probably feel happy that they had a rare day off together. She sat down with a bowl of cornflakes and stared glassily at the screen as Ed liberated Europe.

Lisa: What do you fancy doing today?

Ed: Just taking it easy.

Lisa: Yeah, but how? What do you want to do?

Ed: Nothing, that's what I mean by taking it easy. I do stuff every day at work. Today I want to do nothing.

Lisa: Don't you want to get away somewhere? It looks

sunny out. We should get out of this place, go somewhere.

Ed: We shouldn't have to do anything. I want to just switch off, shoot Germans, or we could get some videos in if you want, lie on the sofa and eat toast all day.

Lisa: It just seems a bit of a waste.

Ed: Waste of what?

Lisa: Waste of time . . . of life.

Ed: That's the point of life, isn't it? To waste time until you die. You have to waste the time.

Lisa stopped listening and looked out at the blue sky. She kept looking until she felt the urge to scream go away. She knew she always did this, always got into a state on her days off. She idealized time away from work to such an extent that it could never live up to her expectations. She scrutinized every minute, trying to evaluate if it represented the optimal use of her time, until she became paralysed with indecision and anxiety. She couldn't sit still. She got up and tried to think of something good to do, but there was nothing left, she'd been on every day trip in a fifty-mile radius. She'd tried day trips to other cities, long walks in the hills, rainy afternoons in dismal market towns, safari parks, art galleries . . . and Ed would always say, 'Why is that less of a waste of time than relaxing at home?' and she never had an answer.

Ed thought the problem was their flat. He kept on at Lisa to go and look at the new loft apartments they were building by the canal. He said maybe she'd enjoy time at home if they lived in one of those, and maybe she could face work if she had somewhere nice to come home to. He described a luxury lifestyle sipping chilled white wine on the balcony. Lisa imagined the balcony view of Green Oaks – a panorama of the glue sniffers who liked to get wasted on the roof. She imagined living in the shadow of the centre, being saddled with a mortgage, but thought maybe she was just refusing to grow up. She had agreed to go and see the cheapest – though still reassuringly expensive – apartment later in the week.

She saw it was half ten and felt the panic that her day off was slipping away already. She was trying not to think about the parcel she was expecting in the post. Lisa had a superstition that if you waited for something to happen – a parcel to arrive, a phone to ring, a saviour to come – then it never happened. You had to not care, you had to be looking the other way, then it would be all right. All week she'd been failing to put the parcel from her brother out of her mind; every day it was the first thing she thought of. She gave up trying to forget about it for today.

'Has there been any post?'

Ed continued shooting Germans. 'Dunno, I haven't passed the door yet. Why do you keep asking about the post?'

'It's just we haven't had any for days.'

'And you're missing being told that there's a large cash prize awaiting you?'

'I was expecting a birthday present.'

Ed shifted his attention from the screen and looked at Lisa. 'Your birthday was last week. Or do you have two like the queen?'

'I know when my birthday was. There was a present I was expecting that didn't come and I'm just worried it might have got lost in the post.'

'You didn't like my present, did you? I knew you didn't.'

'What are you talking about? I'm not talking about your present. I'm expecting something else, from someone else.'

'Yeah, but clearly you're anxious about it, worried you might have missed it. I bet you wouldn't care if you hadn't got mine.'

'Well, as yours was a CD from Your Music, had it got lost, I wouldn't have too much difficulty in replacing it.'

'Is it a crime to get your present from Your Music? Would it be a better present if I'd gone to another shop, spent hours wandering around town not having a clue what to get you?'

Lisa didn't have the energy to answer this truthfully, she wasn't prepared to enter the kind of territory it might lead to. 'No, the CD is great. I like it. I wasn't being funny.'

'Just cos Dan bought you some poncey book on photography it doesn't mean he thought about it any more than I did.'

'No, I know,' Lisa lied.

'So who's this present you're waiting for off?'

'My brother.'

Ed was lost in France again, dealing with some snipers at the upper window of an abandoned café. 'I didn't know you had a brother,' he murmured.

'I don't really,' Lisa said.

She forced herself to accept that maybe a walk by the canal might be nice.

*

Kurt was watching a man who might or might not have been the Green Oaks lift-shitter. Four years into his campaign and still no one had identified him. Security guards spoke of him in awe: the lift was glass-sided – how did he do it unnoticed? Some said he brought it with him but Kurt believed it was the act, not the product, that was the motivation. Now he watched as a man in a grey coat with classic joke-shop milk-bottle glasses went up and down in the lift repeatedly. Kurt had noticed that as the doors opened on each level, the man tried to close them quickly before anyone else got in.

Kurt's attention was distracted by the sighting of Blind Dave on level 2 and the consequent need to alert other security staff. Blind Dave was a regular Green Oaks visitor, and a man who challenged the cliché that blind people have some semi-supernatural ability to find their way about and intuit presences around them. Dave walked into most obstacles in his path, and was given to embracing desperately any upright fixed object in front of him like a man adrift for weeks. He flailed his white stick at knee height and thus generally failed to detect the approach of stairs and other ground-level features. On two occasions he had disappeared over the edge of the stairs on level 3. When standing still, Dave tended to rock back and forth quite violently and one time, seemingly unaware that he was in front of the central fountain, rocked forward so hard that he teetered on the wall of the pool, before tipping head first into it. There was a strong suspicion amongst security staff that Dave was in fact not blind at all and as Kurt watched him now, it seemed to him that Dave's eyes were apparently very focused on a PlayStation in the window of Dixons. After a moment Dave seemed to remember himself and stepped forward to bang his head loudly on the window. Kurt watched him as he made his terrifying progress along the main promenade. The crowds parted and a thirty-foot clear radius opened up around him. A woman standing at the cashpoint machine was oblivious to his imminent collision with her.

Kurt remembered it was his birthday and sighed. He knew exactly how many he had passed in Green Oaks, and wondered how many more he would spend there. He thought back to his job interview thirteen years ago. As he was led up to the security office, the young guard with big ears showing him the way told him bluntly that it was a shit job with shit wages and that Green Oaks was the biggest shithole of all. He told him to go to college and get a better job. Kurt shrugged. He was seventeen with no qualifications. In the year since he'd left school the lack of employers queuing up and knocking on his door had been conspicuous.

In the week leading up to Kurt's O Levels, his father suffered a brain haemorrhage. Kurt missed his exams, and stayed at home with his mom for a few months trying to help her care for Kurt Sr. So it was his father's own doing that led Kurt to end up working at Green Oaks. There had been no other option. Money was a priority.

Kurt couldn't clearly remember his first visit to Green Oaks. He remembered planning it as a mission for one of his truant days. He remembered his desire to walk where his father had worked. The factory had seemed so vivid to Kurt that he couldn't quite believe all trace could be wiped away. He was sure in some corner or basement he'd find some blackened tools or some rusted valve. In later years, as a security guard, he'd seen photos of red plastic Wimpys and prehistoric supermarkets but he had no real recollection of Green Oaks when it opened – it was another blank amongst the many in his head.

Kurt's mother had still never stepped foot in Green Oaks. Obedient as ever to her husband, she was one of the dwindling number who still doggedly visited the few remaining local shops. They were difficult to get to as the bus didn't stop there any more, but Pat would walk the two miles, right past Green Oaks, pulling her tartan trolley behind her up the hill. Kurt often saw her as the bus passed, standing windswept on the kerb, wincing through the fumes as heavy traffic rumbled by. The old High Street was a ghostly place. The doorsteps of the boarded up shops had become favoured haunts for hairspray sniffers and white-cider drinkers. The almost exclusively pensioner clientele was a ready source of easily snatched bags and purses. The local paper had a front-page splash reserved each week for a gruesome extreme close-up of a battered old face, purple and swollen, crosshatched with black stitches, watery eyes furiously burning out of the page. At fifty-five, Pat was perhaps the youngest woman to shop on the High Street, and she was the hero of the pensioners and shopkeepers alike. She wrote letters to the paper and to the council deploring the state of the street. She badgered the police about the street drinkers. She accompanied terrified pensioners on their shopping trips, or offered to do their shopping for them.

Kurt's father, meanwhile, sat propped up at home in his Parker Knoll, oblivious to all this sacrifice on his behalf. His haemorrhage had rendered him paralysed and seemingly insensible. No one knew exactly how much, if anything, he took in of the world around him. He gave no clues, but sitting rigid, staring straight ahead, he still generated the power and strange menace he always had. Kurt found his presence terrifying. He felt his father knew of his job. He could feel his contempt for his stupid uniform, for his walking around all day doing nothing but watching over women's clothes and chasing children. His father had done hard physical work all his life, for what? For his wife to contend with drug addicts and criminals while trying to find the cheapest cut of meat and for his son to go slowly out of his mind earning £4.25 an hour.

Kurt's attention was drawn back to the lift where the man in milk-bottle glasses was attempting to escape as Blind Dave entered flailing his stick, and the doors closed behind them.

21

She locked the back door and made her way back through the service corridors and out into the main body of the centre. It was a late finish. The computer had a headache or something – it wouldn't generate the day's figures and Lisa had been stuck trying to coax them out. She never did the clandestine routine at night. At night she just wanted to leave. She leaned against a dull grey door hidden in the wall of dull grey breeze blocks and emerged on the other side through the mirrored surface of the west mall.

The lights were dimmed and when she reached the customer entrance to the car parks she found it locked. She looked around the half-lit mall and felt a small shock of panic. She had never been there so late before on her own. There was no Radio Green Oaks, no hum of buffing machines, no sound at all. Instead there were unfamiliar angles and shadows, and the air felt cold.

She knew there were fire exits out through the service corridors. She had a dim memory of some complicated route to the car park that she and some other late workers had taken one night after a stocktake, but she couldn't remember the way now. She decided to walk down to the fountain where the security guards tended to congregate in the daytime. Hopefully one would be patrolling round there now and she could get him to unlock the door for her.

She walked past the darkened shop fronts and saw inside the disarray of frenzied shopping – filmy party tops trampled on the carpet, left-footed trainers jumbled on floors, empty crisp bags in CD racks. She was missing the indistinct chiming of canned music. She wondered who it was who thought to put it on so early in the morning, and why they turned it off at night. She liked the music in the morning: it made everything seem a little unreal. She knew she'd feel better if she could hear it now.

She reached the fountain: no sign of any guard. She felt the pulse of fear start somewhere inside and tried to calm herself down. She thought of her morning pantomimes and realized that she would look genuinely suspicious if a security guard spotted her now, and she was scared of being picked up by one of the cameras. She would explain about the locked door, but she imagined them not believing her, searching her bag, assuming that, far from leaving, she had in fact let herself back into the centre with her keys in order to steal stock from the store.

Lisa grew sure that she was being watched; she felt visible in a way that was frightening. Someone was watching, but they weren't coming to help. She was being observed and assessed. She headed back to the mirrored door and decided to take her chances trying to find the route to the car park through the service corridors. She wanted to get away from the cameras, to become invisible again.

Forty increasingly desperate minutes later, she spotted the back of a security guard disappearing around a corner way ahead of her in the grey corridor. Her paranoia was now outweighing her desperation to escape the labyrinth and she hung back, hoping she could follow him unseen until he led her to an exit. She kept well behind the guard and tried to take steps identical to his. As she followed him she started to feel calmer. His silhouette reminded her of her brother. The fear faded and she felt more in control, more like the slick terrorist she played every morning. She was the watcher now.

*

It was sometime around eleven when Kurt stopped patrolling suddenly and held his breath. He strained the muscles in his face and tried to listen. He tried to hear beyond the faint buzz of the fluorescent strip, beyond the even fainter sounds of ventilation fans, but there was nothing at all. He had been lost in his thoughts and couldn't tell how long he had been aware of the presence. He walked on, behaving as only someone who thinks they are being watched can behave. He never considered walking back the way he had come; something about that idea was unappealing enough to not even cross his mind. He knew he could press his walkie-talkie button and call Scott. He knew someone was walking behind him.

He turned and looked back up the grey passage again, but there was nothing to see. Turning round had been a bad idea. The sight of the long empty corridor scared him badly. He knew it wasn't empty: something was hiding. He carried on walking, trying to insinuate himself back into the distraction of whatever he'd been thinking about, but he couldn't get a grip. Twice more he stopped and listened and looked, and twice more nothing materialized.

Maybe only three or four minutes had passed when Kurt finally turned and called, 'Is anybody there?' and the girl emerged from behind a girder twenty feet back, with a monkey in a suit hanging from her bag.

22

Lisa emerged from behind the pipe. The guard looked less like her brother from the front – just a similar build. He seemed nervous.

She wasn't sure what to say, and so after a moment's silence her first words to him were: 'I'm lost.' She started to explain what had happened and how she'd been trying to get home, but trailed off as she realized that he wasn't listening to her but was staring at the stuffed monkey she had attached to her bag.

'Where did you get that?' he said.

'I found it in the service corridor. It was stuffed behind a pipe. Maybe I shouldn't have moved it. I just liked the look of it . . .' She fell quiet for a moment and then added brightly, 'He's got spats.' She was conscious of sounding like an idiot. She'd been frightened on her own and now she was talking too much. She half recognized the guard's face from around the centre. Still he stared at the monkey and said nothing.

'You're scaring me a bit,' Lisa said eventually. This seemed to rouse him from his thoughts.

'I'm sorry. You scared me too. I've seen that monkey before. I think it belongs to a little girl. I saw her one night on the monitor. Maybe she's been back since. Maybe she comes and hides here at night – brings her monkey with her.' Kurt trailed off into thought. After a moment or two Lisa cleared her throat and he spoke again: 'I've just got a feeling that I should have tried harder to find her. Maybe she's in trouble.' The guard closed his eyes. Lisa looked at his face. She recognized his tiredness, but beyond that there was sadness. She worried for a moment that he'd actually fallen asleep. She reached out to touch his shoulder and he opened his eyes.

'You should try and find her,' she said. 'Maybe she's run away from home . . .' She paused for a moment and thought about her brother. She found herself saying, 'I'll help you if you like. She might be less scared of a woman. We could find her and talk to her. This is a horrible place to be in by yourself.'

He looked at her. 'Why do you want to help me?'

Lisa wasn't sure what to say, and so told the truth: 'Because I've been lost here for years – maybe you have too – but we could rescue her.'

The guard led her to the exit.

*

Two nights later Kurt waited by the fountain. She said she'd be out of work by around 10.30. He told Scott that she had asked for a tour around the service corridors so she didn't get lost again.

She turned up and they walked along the grey lanes looking for any signs of human life, any signs of child activity. Kurt walked here every night and really didn't know what they expected to find: signs to guide them like in a fairy tale, a trail of toffee wrappers maybe. Lisa had a bag of sweets and was placing them where she thought the child might see them. With each sweet she had written a note saying: 'I think I have your monkey. Come to Your Music and ask for Lisa.' Kurt was worried other guards might find these and infer some erotic intent, but he said nothing.

They were awkward in each other's company and their conversation was mannered. They talked about the child, who she might be and why she was hiding in the centre. Kurt told Lisa exactly what he'd seen. Their conjecture steered a certain path; neither seemed to have a taste for grim reality. Kurt said maybe she was the leader of a gang of Dickensian child thieves who lived in the ventilation shafts stealing hankerchiefs and fob watches from the fancy folk of Green Oaks. Lisa said maybe she was an eccentric trillionaire dwarf who owned Green Oaks and countless other retail/leisure megaplexes around the globe. Kurt said maybe she'd been abandoned at birth in the centre and had been raised by a community of rats in the service corridors. Lisa said maybe the notebook indicated she was just an incredibly avaricious child spending all day and night making a supremely comprehensive Christmas list.

Kurt relaxed a little. It was strange not to be patrolling alone, but he quite liked the company. He wondered what Lisa thought of his shoes; he wondered if he could ask her for an opinion.

It was one o'clock when they reached the waste area. The corridor bloomed open into a sunken hangar-like space filled with vast containers for all of Green Oaks' waste. During the day Eric and Tone were in charge down here. They guarded the containers officiously and divided their realm in bizarre and minute ways no one but them could fathom. Polystyrene peanut packaging went in one container, non-peanut shapes another; flat plastic wrap went in one, bubble wrap another; usually food and litter went in together, as did wood and metal, but some days a change in policy would make this the very worst thing to do. The coalitions and divergences of the different waste groupings seemed to shift daily, and it was entirely feasible that Eric and Tone were making it all up to amuse themselves. Kurt often stopped and had a chat with them on his rounds, but as they talked Eric and Tone would keep a close eye on shop drones laboriously vivisecting various boxes and crates, to ensure their law was upheld.

Occasionally a new or insane Green Oaks employee would fling unbroken boxes, display stands and bin bags in the first container they came to, with dramatic results. Tone actually had a whistle to sound the alarm. The perpetrator would be apprehended with unnecessary violence and dragged back to the containers. Eric would scream, 'What the fuck do you think you are doing? What the fuck do you think you are doing?' over and over, while the perpetrator, now in the container with the misfiled rubbish, would be silently shown exactly where each of the constituent waste elements should be taken, by means of Grim Reaper-style pointing from Tone. Eric and Tone called it zero tolerance. Eighteen months previously one such rogue tipper had managed to outrun Eric and Tone and escaped into the labyrinth. Hand-drawn 'Wanted' posters still festooned the bay. The furious sketches of some fleeing deformed homunculus vividly captured Eric and Tone's sense of violation, but the lack of resemblance to human form rendered them ineffective as a means of identification.

Eric and Tone had constructed a kind of shanty town next to the containers, consisting of two principal shacks and various outbuildings, all made from old display racks, cardboard cut-outs of past attractions and pre-refit carpets. Here they would sit out in front of the shacks on salvaged chairs, looking like homesteaders rocking on their porches, surveying their land. It was hard to imagine Eric and Tone existing outside their lair, but every evening at six o'clock sharp they left for their real homes and, even more unbelievably, their families.

It was late and Lisa and Kurt were tired of walking. Neither of them had really expected to find the girl on their first search, but they'd made a start. Maybe she'd see Lisa's notes. Maybe she'd gone back to wherever she came from.

Kurt felt calmer now that he'd done something. He sat down with Lisa on the makeshift porch as if admiring the view and said, 'I guess maybe she's gone back home now.'

'Yeah – I suppose that's a good thing.'

'Yeah, anywhere must be better than here.'

'I don't know – I suppose if you're very unhappy at home, anywhere is better than there.'

Kurt looked at her. 'Did you ever have to run away from home?'

Lisa looked at the ground. 'Yeah, once.'

'How old were you?'

'Eight.'

Kurt didn't think he should ask why. 'Where did you go?'

'I hid in the garden.'

'Oh . . . so you didn't actually leave home then.'

'Yeah. The garden was massive and I was right down the end of it behind a hedge. I'd packed a carrier bag of socks and taken them with me.'

'Just socks?'

'I forgot about the other stuff. I knew there was stuff you had to change every day but I couldn't remember what it was.'

Kurt stared at Lisa for a while and then asked: 'Were your parents worried?'

'They didn't even know I'd gone. I left a note explaining my reasons, but my mom came out to the garden to hang out some washing and found me before she saw the note.'

'What were your reasons?'

'That for the millionth time she had bought mint-flavoured Viscount biscuits rather than proper YoYos, even though I always said I didn't like the Viscounts and that they weren't the same.'

'You left because of biscuits?'

'No, not just the biscuits – what they represented.'

'What was that?'

'Neglect.'

'It sounds pretty bad.'

'You know the worst thing?'

'No.'

'The worst thing was what my mom said when she saw me.'

'Right.'

'Some of the socks had spilled from the carrier bag and she saw me and she said, "Ooh, are you having a picnic with your friends?"'

'She thought the socks were your friends?'

'Worse than that – she thought that I thought that the socks were my friends. She thought that's how clueless I was.'

'Oh dear,' said Kurt.

'Exactly,' said Lisa. 'Let's change the subject now.'

Disc Jockey
Radio Green Oaks Studio

Shhhhhhh. Quiet, sweetheart. Strictly speaking we're not supposed to be in here this late at night. I thought it'd be nice to come somewhere a little quieter though, didn't you? Have a bit of privacy? Have a bit of conversation?

It's funny, isn't it, how you can just meet someone and hit it off with them? I felt something when I saw you tonight. No, I don't mean like that. I thought you'd be a good listener. You've got nice eyes, kind eyes. What are you laughing for? I mean it. It's not just a line.

I haven't always been the voice of Radio Green Oaks, you know. Maybe you're a little young to remember: I worked at Radio Wyvern Sound for fifteen years, various shows, but most people remember me for the final eight years there, when I did Romantica. *It was a big show, ten till midnight every weekday night – maybe too late for you back then. It had the second highest listening figures after the breakfast show, and no one at Wyvern came close in terms of listener calls.*

'Can you play "Air that I Breathe" by the Hollies for my girlfriend Sarah, cos I love her more than I can ever tell her.'

'Please can you dedicate "Alone Again (Naturally)" by Gilbert O'Sullivan to my ex-girlfriend Jessica. It's been three years now, Jessica, but I still love you and want you to know I'm waiting.'

'I want to request "Reunited" for my princess Meena. Tell her it will never happen again and I want her to forgive me.'

'Please play "Close to You" for David and tell him that he is the only glue that can fix my broken heart.'

We got more requests than we could ever get through. So much activity of the heart directed straight into my earpiece. Can you imagine that? Maybe you're too young to understand. I was a lightning conductor for all this electricity. All these invisible currents that were shooting out across the Wyvern region – I caught them all. It was hard to sleep at night knowing what was going on out there. I'd close my eyes and I'd feel the irregular beating of all these disturbed hearts. But my heart was not disturbed, my heart was still, so still I started to think that maybe I was dead.

Every night I dreamt of a place – do you know where I mean? Have you had that dream? Every night I dreamt of a place and I knew the place was death, and I'd wake up wringing with sweat, and there as I lay on the damp sheets I'd feel my limp heart beating just enough to tell me I was still alive.

The station bosses were deciding whether to shunt Glenn Rydale off the weekend nightspots and extend Romantica *to seven days a week. It felt that even if we ran* Romantica

24/7 we still wouldn't get through all the requests – lovesickness seemed to be spreading. I think my heart was the only heart in Wyvern that was still.

Then more suddenly than I think you could imagine, it all stopped. Two weeks. That's not a long time, is it? In two weeks we went from total system overload to nothing. Friday 11th March 1983 – no one called. Some massive cardiac arrest, a monstrous coronary atrophy, ten thousand hearts silenced. I tried to bring them round, I pumped on the chest, I played songs that would make the dead weep, but the corpse was cold. Love was dead, and I never felt more alive. Can you understand that?

I lost my job, obviously, but within months I became the voice of Green Oaks. I never saw it as a step down. I tell the people of Green Oaks that spring is here, I tell them forty-nine shopping days till Christmas – perhaps you've heard me say that – I tell them that this season we're looking to the East for inspiration – and I don't feel dead. I tell them to enjoy two meals for the price of one in the food court before 12.30 and does anybody feel their heart beating strangely today? I ask if they ever phoned Romantica *to request a song for the person standing beside them, who once took up their entire field of vision and now they can barely even see. I ask them if they ever got drunk and left a bar with a man twice their age and fell asleep with their head in his dormant lap. I ask them if they've considered the many advantages of a Green Oaks credit card and do they ever wonder what happened to love? I ask them all these things, sweetheart, but I never hear the answers.*

23

Kurt thought he looked a lot better in the darkened glass of the office than in real life. He was more tanned, more hollow. He moved his head from side to side, trying to get a new angle on his reflected face, trying to surprise himself, trying to see past his own eyes. When he got bored with that he started playing with the ball of tinfoil on the desk. The tinfoil ball was a true friend on these long nights. Bin practice always killed about fifteen or twenty minutes, or until he just got fed up of retrieving the ball. The thing that made getting the ball in the bin great wasn't the final payoff, not the actual docking, but the unerring sense as the ball left his hand that it was going to hit the target. It was a small feeling, but a good one. A voice in the head saying something as simple as 'yes' for a change.

Last week he had found a new way of fun with foil. Not fun really, just the murder of time. He would break a tiny bit of foil off and make a micro-sized ball, but with still enough heft to fly through the air adequately. Then with his eyes shut he would spin around in his swivel chair, until at some point he hurled the tiny silver cluster somewhere out into the office, shooting through the silent carpeted universe. Anything up to an hour could then be spent methodically searching the room for the particle. Sometimes he'd imagine he was looking for a fallen meteor ('excitement mounts'), at others a serial killer ('the net closes in'), at others still that it was a missing child ('hope is fading'). Tonight, though, he felt tired and listless and the foil just couldn't excite him enough.

He turned to the monitors again and flicked through the different vistas. There were twenty-four screens, each one able to display eight different camera mountings, giving Kurt 192 different still lives of Green Oaks at 3.17 a.m. this March night.

The escalators were still and the same murky half-light extended from the silent butcher's in the basement to the hundreds of empty chairs arranged neatly in the food court on the top floor. Nothing living: no people, no dogs, no flies – only the rats in the service corridors, Scott out in the car parks and him here in his luxurious leather swivel chair.

He was thinking about loneliness when he saw her again. On screen 6, by the banks, where she had been last time. He zoomed in, not moving his eyes from her. He was so scared she'd disappear again he whispered into his radio: 'Scott, Scott.'

Scott's response came crackling loudly back: 'All right, Kurt, mate. You got the kettle on?'

'Scott, the girl. She's in the centre again. I've got her right on camera on level 2 by the banks.'

'You serious, mate?'

'She's standing there looking at the door to the bank.'

'OK, I'll go up and see what the story is.'

'All right, go quietly though in case she hears you and runs. Scott, don't scare her.'

'All right, just keep watching her.'

Kurt could see in the corner of his eye Scott moving across the screens from the car park. The different angles and placings of the cameras made his progress erratic. Sometimes he seemed to be moving closer to her and then on the next monitor he'd be walking away. She had the notebook again and Kurt was surprised to see that she still had the monkey sticking out of her bag. Lisa must have found something else. Something about her seemed familiar. Kurt knew he'd seen her before. Maybe he'd seen her on the day shift. He zoomed in more, but he still couldn't get a clear view of her face. She was wearing a camouflage jacket too big for her, and she looked intent on something. She didn't look like someone on the run, but Kurt felt scared for her.

The radio crackled again, and this time Scott was whispering. 'Kurt, I'm on level 1 now, I think it's best if I go up through the service stairs to the next floor. She'll hear me otherwise. I'll come out the door by HSBC.'

'That's perfect, you'll be right in front of her there – you'll be able to catch her if she runs.'

Kurt adjusted the angle of the camera a tiny amount, so that the mirrored door from which Scott would emerge was visible in the corner of the screen with the girl. He felt that he'd let her down by not finding her last time, he felt he owed her something; he wanted to help her. He waited fifteen, twenty, thirty seconds and then the door opened slowly and Scott emerged directly in front of the girl. She didn't move. She hardly seemed to see him, though there was no mistaking his fifteen-stone form. Kurt noticed himself shaking. For his part Scott seemed hesitant. He edged a couple of steps towards her and then stopped. Kurt watched him raise his radio to his mouth, and wondered why he was wasting time.

'Kurt, give me some more instructions.'

'Just speak to her, what else can I say?'

'Where is she? I mean, which way did she go?'

'Are you blind? She's standing in front of you.'

At last, Scott walked a few feet forward until he was just a few inches from the girl, who still hadn't moved.

'There, now you got her. Ask her her name, tell her everything's all right. She looks frozen to the spot.'

But Scott didn't talk to the girl. Instead he turned around slowly, as if he was scared to move too fast, tilted his head upwards towards the camera and said, 'There's nobody here, mate.'

24

She kept her foot on the accelerator, revving the engine even though the traffic hadn't moved in minutes. The engine was highly strung, hysterical even, demanding constant reassurance. Any decrease in pressure on the accelerator and the engine would flounce out of the negotiations: cut out instantly. You had to keep reassuring it: look, there's plenty of petrol, here's some more and some more . . . move away from the ledge. It made braking difficult. Lisa had perfected a kind of stuttering halt, where she rapidly switched her foot between brake and accelerator, keeping the revs up while slowing down.

She watched the yellow smear of Millennium Balti's neon sign dissolve slowly and slide down her windscreen. Was the protracted argument over Terry-Thomas last night? Or was that the night before? She remembered Matt almost screaming, 'There's no fucking hyphen!' but not much else. There were snatches of a conversation in the toilet about dogs, but she didn't remember with who, or why. Dan had at some point done what he seemed to see as his duty as Lisa's best friend and delivered his usual lecture about Ed: why was she wasting her life with a self-mythologizing, lazy, lying twat, was the general gist if she remembered rightly. She would defend Ed, but never really knew the answer to his questions. Now she found her mind kept drifting and thinking about the security guard and their nocturnal walk around the centre. The wipers erased the colour seepage and Millennium Balti was restored.

She wasn't going to drink whisky again. So with vodka and gin previously vowed off, that meant venturing into the more exotic territories of rums and brandies. White rum. That's not too weird, is it? Bacardi and Coke – a bit early 1980s but that's OK. Would the Eagle sell Bacardi? Lisa couldn't reconcile the image of Havana and the Eagle.

Built in the 1960s, the Eagle was a sprawling beige-brick bungalow attempting some kind of country hostelry feel with dimpled glass and skinny beams. This aspiration was disastrously undermined by the immense Third Reich-style relief eagle that dominated the front of the pub. More Berchtesgaden than village inn. It was here in the orange back room that much of the Your Music staff could be found on any night. No one else seemed to use the pub. Locals deserted it when a low-price chain pub opened at Green Oaks. Your Music staff went there because it was the only pub in a mile's radius of the centre and because of the vast and strangely arcane jukebox selection that they could argue over. Professor Longhair then Esther Williams then the Louvin Brothers . . .

Six months ago Lisa had forced herself, in a rare moment of resolve, to write a list of just a few of the better ways to spend an evening than sitting in the Eagle. It read:

1. see some non-Your Music friends
2. read a book
3. go to the cinema
4. do charitable work
5. concentrate hard and try and remember what it is I wake up thinking every morning but instantly forget
6. bake a cake
7. decide on hairstyle strategy
8. look for other jobs
9. visit Mom and Dad

10. remove brown stain on kitchen wall that always makes me sad
11. take a walk around the city at night
12. take some photos
13. listen to the CDs I buy but never listen to
14. think about something
15. talk to Ed.

But every night after another shitty day at work she was filled with an urge that would not be denied to go to the orange back room and get lost in a blur of words and faces and alcohol. The room where everything was so fucking hilarious, and where time whipped by at ten times its normal awful speed. She enjoyed spending time with Dan. It wasn't, as Ed might sometimes insinuate, that anything was going on. Dan was her oldest friend and Lisa liked the fact that he'd known her before she worked at Your Music. Lisa felt as if Dan knew a better version of her – someone with interests and ideas and plans. All that was best about Lisa, or had once been best, was saved in Dan's memory and had yet to be overwritten by the newer, paler reality. The same was also true in reverse. They both had high hopes for each other, if not for themselves.

Ed never went to the Eagle. He pretended to be oblivious to Dan's hatred, but he avoided him all the same, and Lisa wished that once he might come and be nice and prove Dan wrong. Instead he stayed at home and played on his turntables or went out with his permatanned friends to clubs which played the kind of white dance music that Lisa hated. And tonight Lisa was stuck in this traffic but at least she was going home and not leaving her car to go to the Eagle. Home, where she knew Ed wasn't, and that was fine because tonight she might bake a cake or remove a stain, and after that she might think about something.

*

Scott wouldn't work with him on the night shift now. In fact no one would except Gavin. Scott had been scared that night. He wasn't sure what was scarier, standing within inches of a ghost, or being trapped alone in the centre for five more hours with Kurt.

Word had got around the other guards and everyone was treating Kurt as if he had the shining. Kurt himself didn't know what to make of it. He wasn't scared, but he was unsettled. Only two people seemed unfazed by the incident (as it was now referred to): Gavin, his new night partner, and Jeff the boss.

Jeff had insisted Kurt take a few days off. He put it all down to fatigue: too many night shifts in a row. 'Sometimes when you're knackered, you think you're awake, you even look and sound as if you're awake, but you're off in a dream. It's the same with the wife. I've seen her get up and start making a Sunday lunch in the middle of the night. You can talk to her while she's doing it, and it's as if she's wide awake, but you know she's miles away. The other night we were sitting in bed talking about the extension completely normally, and all of a sudden she shouts out: "It was Wogan! He ate all the peas – I saw the greedy devil," and I realized she'd been asleep for God knows how long.'

Kurt had a momentary unhappy flash of what life must be like for Jeff's wife. They had been having their extension built for the past eighteen months. Jeff spoke about it a lot, enough for Kurt to understand Mrs Jeff seeking refuge in a dreamworld.

Jeff carried on: 'That's all it was. You were asleep, you were dreaming. Don't take any notice of the others. Scott's shaken up, it's understandable. It scares me sometimes when she's there looking for a leg of lamb in the wardrobe.'

So Kurt spent a few days at home. He reluctantly accepted Jeff's theory. The memory of seeing the child on both occasions had none of the fuzziness or time slippage associated with dreams, but Kurt knew how deceptive they could be. He'd confused dreams and reality in the past; the doctors had said it wasn't so rare. There was something reminiscent of a nightmare about the anxiety he'd felt when he'd seen her. He was alarmed that he was still experiencing lapses like this. He wondered to what extent he'd really got over his sleep problem in the last few years. How often was he asleep and yet remembering stuff as if he was awake?

While he was at home he decided to act on his forgotten resolution. He had to find a job where he wasn't so isolated, and he wasn't on shifts. He was tired of hiding from life at Green Oaks. It was doing him no good.

And so Kurt spent his nights now with Gavin. Gavin, like Kurt, was not one of the lads – he didn't go out for beers, he didn't zoom the cameras in on women's breasts, he kept quiet and went home every evening to his wife. Gavin looked as if sunlight had never touched him. His hair was fine pale ginger and his skin was milky white. There was something about his staring blue eyes that reminded Kurt of Jerry Lee Lewis. His facial expression always seemed on the brink of terrible fury or wicked humour, neither of which he ever came close to manifesting. Kurt had never actually heard him speak until the first evening they worked together, when Gavin spoke a lot. Kurt thought perhaps it was a special effort by Gavin to keep him awake and alert. But Gavin's soft, barely audible voice and his choice of subject matter made for a poor stimulant, and twice during Gavin's first-night monologue, Kurt felt his head bob heavily. The same monologue continued more or less, with little thematic deviation, every subsequent night as well. Gavin could talk for hour after hour. Kurt had never known nights like them. The time between one and four seemed to stretch for days. No matter how long he patrolled the car parks or the service corridors he knew that Gavin was waiting for him back in the control room, ready to serve out more of his soft, slow torture.

Gavin had one theme, one passion, one abiding fascination: Green Oaks.

Kurt learned that Gavin had worked at Green Oaks since it opened back in 1983. He seemed to see himself as curator of the centre – tending its history, dusting its artefacts. Gavin would sometimes pronounce, 'I know all its secrets,' and Kurt would clench his fist around his ball of tinfoil and realize that in time he would know them all too, and he knew already that none of them was worth knowing.

Kurt learned that Green Oaks was one of the first new-generation shopping centres in the country, not to be confused with the first wave/old generation of Arndales and Bull Rings (incidentally did he realize how many Arndale centres there were in the UK?). He learned it was the first to be built on a brownfield site away from a city centre, and even now, at 1.5 million square foot, it remained the largest in the country. He learned that an average of 497,000 shoppers visited in the week before Christmas. He learned that there could be 350 shoppers in the nineteen passenger lifts at any one time He learned that on any given Saturday only six per cent of the shoppers would be unskilled workers. He learned that 100,000 cubic metres of contaminated waste had had to be cleared from the old gasworks. He learned that Green Oaks had twelve miles of service passageways and, just before he was bludgeoned into utter numbness, he felt a final sharp pang of incredulity as he learned that Gavin had in fact spent a night walking the entire length of these twelve miles and recorded the expedition on video. Many a time over the subsequent interminable nights, Kurt would imagine Gavin and his catatonic wife watching four hours of grey corridor footage while Gavin freeze-framed his favourite bits and delivered his commentary.

At times Gavin seemed to talk about Green Oaks as if it were alive. As if somehow the steel, the glass, the concrete and the people combined to make something bigger, something almost worthy of reverence. Gavin had copies of the original plans, he had photographs mapping the centre's changes, rebrands and refits. He was intent on mounting a display of all these in the atrium in the very near future. Did Kurt know why? No he did not, because not many people realized that October 2004 would mark Green Oaks' 21st birthday. Not many people seemed to think it worth marking. Not many people knew all its secrets.

25

Lisa was sitting in Crawford's swivel chair, not looking forward to the next half hour. There was a knock at the door and in came Steve, the volatile Easy Listening buyer. A man less suited to his chosen genre would be hard to imagine.

Steve: Lisa, do you want to talk to me now?

Lisa: Yeah, Steve. I've got Mike to cover you on the counter.

Steve: So is it about what happened the other day?

Lisa: Yes, it is.

Steve: OK, OK. Well, give me the disciplinary or whatever and I'll take it. I don't want to lose my job. I work hard here, I keep my section right, but some of these people, Lees, they're playing with us, do you know what I mean? They're fucking with us.

Lisa: I know, I know. But I suppose you've got to try not to let it get to you so personally.

Steve: It was a one-off.

Lisa: Well, it was and it wasn't. I mean, it was the first time you actually struck a customer, but it wasn't really the first time you let one get to you.

Steve: I did not strike him. I tried to explain this to the motherfucker while he was screaming assault. I said, 'Brother, if I had assaulted you, you would know.'

Lisa: Look, Steve, look. We can talk about what happened, but I want us to establish right from the start that you have a history of being perhaps a little highly strung with customers, or else we're not really being honest about the situation. Can we agree on that?

Steve: Well, Lisa, I want to co-operate. Like I say, I like my job. I appreciate you doing this disciplinary rather than Crawford. I know you must have had to persuade him not to sack me on the spot. But I don't think I can agree to that. I would describe myself as 'unusually tolerant'.

Lisa: Steve, remember we often have lunch together, remember I'm often there trying to eat my sandwich when you're letting off a little steam, often for the entire hour. Do you remember the guy last week?

Steve: There were many guys last week. Every week there are many guys who come, all looking to make their point with Steve.

Lisa: Right. Well, the guy I'm talking about was the guy looking for the Ray Conniff CD.

Steve: Oh yeah, oh yeah, exactly what I'm talking about.

Lisa: No, this is exactly what I'm talking about. It was not a big deal, you were being paranoid.

Steve: Lisa, he watched me, he watched me take that CD off the rack and put it in the crate to be returned to the company. He watched me do that and then he watched me put hundreds of other CDs in the case on top of it, then he watched me carry that big crate over to the lift and he waits and waits – and then when I'm standing there with my arms shaking with the effort, he asks me if we have *The Happy Sound of Ray Conniff* by Ray Conniff.

Lisa: Steve, look, I saw the dent in the staff-room wall. You take it all so personally. You had to get your knuckles bandaged after –

Steve: Exactly. I punched the wall, not his face. 'Unusually tolerant'.

Lisa: It suggests a lot of aggression, Steve.

Steve: Look, Lisa – let me tell you about this guy. I'll tell you what happened. I swear I did not assault him. He came up to me and said he supposed I couldn't help, supposed it was a waste of time, but he'd been trying to track a tune down for years – get that, Lisa, remember that: 'for years' – a tune his father used to sing all the time, always just singing the same line over and over again. His dad had died years ago, and now for his mom's eightieth birthday he wanted to find this tune and buy it for her, cos he knew she'd always wanted to hear the full version, had never known what it was. I thought, nice guy, doing something nice for his mom. I said, 'So you don't have an artist or a title,' and he said, 'No, I think it's hopeless, I just have the line.' So I said, 'Well, you're here now, tell me the line,' and he goes, 'The line is "Mr Saturday Dance".'

Lisa: OK.

Steve: So, Lisa. This is the amazing thing. This is the reason I love my job, the reason I care about my job. He could have asked anyone else in this shop about that line, anyone else probably in Green Oaks, and not one of them would have had a clue. But I knew it instantly. Not only did I know it, but I knew he had the line wrong because it was exactly the way I used to mistake the line. It's not 'Mr Saturday Dance' it's 'Missed the Saturday dance'. You see?

Lisa: I don't actually recognize it myself.

Steve: No, OK. Well, most people wouldn't. But I'm not most people. I love my section, it's the music I grew up on. So I say to him, 'It's called "Don't get around much any more", recorded by various artists. I think we have the Ink Spots version in stock.' I have to admit I'm feeling pretty high. This guy has been searching for this track 'for years'. His mom's gonna be made up. So I get the Ink Spots CD – yep, there it is on the back. The CD is budget, only £5.99 – it's all so perfect. I give it to the guy and he says: '£5.99 for one song!?' Do you get that? Not 'Thank you.' Not 'My mother can die happy,' but '£5.99 for one song?'

Lisa: Ah.

Steve: So I say, 'It's not one song, it's an album. Maybe your mother will like other tracks,' and he goes, 'Of black group music! I don't think so.'

Lisa: Black group music? Nice.

Steve: Exactly. Then he says, 'Don't you have it on a single?' Are you hearing this? You know, thirty seconds ago it's his life's quest to even find out what this song is and now he expects it on a single. So I said, still very calm, 'Well, the song was released in 1937, so clearly we don't carry singles from that time.' And that is when he really starts playing with me. He gives a little laugh, a kind of bitter laugh, and says, 'Not such a "superstore" then, are you?' Can you believe this, Lisa? Was he sent from hell? So OK – I admit it – I was a little taken aback by all this –

Lisa: A little taken aback? Is that all?

Steve: Certainly, and so I kind of pushed the CD at him a little and said, 'I think you should take this CD, go to the till and buy it.' And the guy goes, 'At that price? It's daylight robbery!' And so I guess I kind of pushed it again against his chest – well OK, maybe a little higher, maybe his general facial area – and said, maybe a little more urgently, 'Buy it.' So that's when he starts calling assault and bitching about my so-called threatening manner.

Lisa: I see. Look, Steve, I understand, but I'm afraid I think the time has come for a move.

Steve: Oh no, Lisa, don't do it, man. Don't make me go to the stockroom. I'm not like them.

Lisa: Come on, Steve, it will be a break from the customers. It will do you good.

Steve: Lisa, I'm not as bad as those freaks up there. They can't speak, they gibber, it's like *One Flew Over the Cuckoo's Nest*. I've got people skills, I'm the customer service king. Don't put me up there.

Lisa: Sorry, Steve, it's beyond my control. Six months or

so. Keep your head down and the time will pass. I'll visit you.

Steve: Oh, Jesus, help me.

*

Kurt started the night shift patrolling the main walkways of the centre. He had left Gavin in the office listening to static on his radio. Back when Kurt had first noticed that the hissing crackle from Gavin's radio seemed constant, he'd told him to change his radio, assuming it was defective. But Gavin had told him it worked just fine. Since then Kurt had seen Gavin sitting in the office seemingly rapt by what he heard in the white noise.

Kurt tended to daydream more and more now he worked with Gavin. Even though Gavin had recently widened his conversational repertoire to include his knowledge of historic European architecture, it didn't make the time pass any more quickly. Gavin had been on a tour of castles and churches in Germany the previous year and as he imparted key data about the monuments and buildings, Kurt would feel his will to live ebb. Kurt tried to make a space in his head where he could shelter from the fact flow. Sometimes he daydreamed that he was invisible, sometimes that Gavin was in fact a figment of his imagination; last week he had started idly wondering for how long he could defend Green Oaks during a siege. The fantasy had proved so detailed and diverting, so Gavin-proof, that now each night he could retreat into some new corner of the calculations and projections while he patrolled the centre, or even in the office while Gavin statisticized from the swivel chair. Each night he added a little more to the plan and each night the playback lasted a little longer.

Defence took up a lot of his time. If all entrances weren't secured then the siege would be over in hours. He wasn't sure that it would be possible to secure every route in over the course of one night, but that was an assumption he had to go with. Gavin would have to be disposed of somehow – prised off his arse for once and sent out to some urgent mission in the car parks. A siege with Gavin on the inside with him was not a diverting prospect at all and Kurt enjoyed formulating ways of removing his colleague. The DIY superstore would have all he needed to secure or lethally booby-trap every entrance, ventilation shaft and fire escape. Many hours were spent mentally constructing a series of elaborate man-traps at the vast revolving doors, always with Gavin as the human guinea pig testing their efficacy. Camera mountings would be adjusted to cover all potential routes in. There would be peace in the valley. Silence in the food court. Except for the one occupied square foot amid the 1.5 million empty ones – the small space where Kurt would be busily engaged on phase two of the project. Phase two was civil war with Kurt as the agent provocateur. How could the centre most ruthlessly dispatch itself? He tried to imagine a way in which every product and inanimate object in the centre contributed to its own consumption. He would spend weeks, maybe months or years, locked inside Green Oaks laboriously preparing a vast domino fall trail that would culminate with the final implosion of the centre. No, not a domino fall, an enormous scaled version of Mousetrap. A Heath Robinson chain reaction pulling together a thousand discrete events: the clothes soaked in alcohol, the chairs in a vast pyre, the mannequins in the bakery ovens. Kurt would run alongside in his pristine but by now unfashionable clothes, running as fast as he could, trying to be there right at the end.

He was walking through the main atrium thinking about retail Armageddon when he saw Lisa scramble out from under the descending electric shutters of Your Music.

He stood for a minute and watched her fumble with a large bunch of keys, wondering if he should talk to her, and deciding he probably should.

'Hello.'

Lisa jumped a little and turned round. 'I didn't hear you coming. Do you get issued with special silent shoes if you work in security?'

Kurt shook his head. 'These didn't come with the job. I bought them myself.' He looked worriedly at his shoes and asked: 'Do they look like the type of shoes you get free with your job?'

Lisa looked at the shoes too. 'Yes, I'm afraid they do.'

'They look cheap?'

'Well, yes. Sorry.'

'That wasn't really the effect I was after.'

'Were they expensive?'

'No, they were dirt cheap, but I thought they didn't look it.' Kurt seemed disheartened.

Lisa tried to change the subject. 'So, I hear you've been seeing things.'

'Oh, you know about that then.'

'I think everyone does.'

Kurt felt depressed. He thought he'd looked quite gallant that other night as he'd led her out of the shopping centre, thought he'd carried himself quite well on their search. He thought he might have left a good impression, and for some reason he liked that idea.

'What about the monkey, though? Isn't that evidence that she's real?' Lisa asked.

'Well, it doesn't really stand up against Scott's evidence that there was no one in front of him. I think most people would find that more persuasive than the monkey. It's just coincidence. Maybe there are lots of stuffed animals hiding behind pipes in the service corridors – who knows? The girl wasn't there, though: she was a dream.'

'But you were awake?'

'No.' Kurt wished he didn't have to talk about this. 'I thought I was awake, I was acting like I was awake, but I was asleep. I have a sleeping problem.'

'So are you awake now? Or am I a dream?'

'It's hard to tell.'

'If I start growing wings or speaking Russian, will you let me know?'

'OK. Can we talk about your sock friends now instead?'

Lisa smiled.

Kurt had been on his way back to the office to eat his sandwiches, but the thought of Gavin made him ask: 'Are you hungry at all?'

'I'm always hungry after work.'

'Do you need to get home?'

She thought about Ed eating pizza in front of the TV, the flat smelling of pepperoni. She shook her head.

'Come with me then.' Kurt led the way along the mall up to the main atrium. They ascended the escalators to the third floor, which was made up of food outlets around a central seating area – a gallery or a court or a terrazzo, depending on which branding you first knew it as. As they glided up the escalators Lisa found the centre almost beautiful. There was something magical in the vast halls, the half light, the silent motion of the escalators. She bent her head back and looked up through the glass ceiling panels at the black sky above them and saw the blinking wing lights of a plane pass slowly by.

Kurt pointed at a camera and whispered, 'Smile at Gavin, he's watching us.'

When they reached the top floor, he asked, 'What do you fancy: Japanese, Italian, Thai, Mexican . . . ?'

Lisa smiled and said, 'Do you do this every night?'

'I've never done it before. Never occurred to me. I normally have fishpaste sandwiches and listen to Gavin talk about different glazing contractors through the history of Green Oaks.'

Lisa looked at him. The first fellow fishpaste-eater she had ever encountered – out and proud, not hiding the habit away.

'So what do you think?' he asked again.

She thought for a while. 'Which concession might be able to provide a fried egg sandwich?'

He smiled and headed off for the first kitchen to find the ingredients.

Ten minutes later they sat at the one lit table with their sandwiches, surrounded by upturned chairs and darkness. Kurt had made Lisa some chocolate milkshake, but he'd got the formula wrong and she was giving herself a headache trying to suck the thick goo up the straw.

She stopped eventually and said, 'I can't stop thinking about pandas. I saw a programme about them on telly last night and it really depressed me.'

'Why?'

'They have a terrible existence, you know? They spend their lives looking for leaves and bamboo to eat, but eating that stuff does them no good, they can't digest it, so they have no energy. They have to lie down and rest all the time. Just talking about it makes me sad. They're so . . . lost. They spend their whole lives in this pointless pursuit that just saps them.'

'That sounds familiar.'

'I know, I think that's why I got so depressed. Wasting their lives looking for bamboo when what they need is a Mars bar.'

'Sometimes I imagine that I'm the subject of some nature documentary for another species. I think of them watching me spending my life walking around empty corridors and checking doors are locked. I try to imagine the commentary. I think they'd be baffled.'

They were silent for a few minutes and then he added, 'The thing is, even when I'm not thinking about nature documentaries, I still feel like I'm being watched. Do you get that?'

Lisa thought how she felt every morning as she walked through the monitored malls. 'Yeah, at times.'

Kurt hesitated, then continued: 'I get scared here sometimes on my own. I feel I'm being watched – not just by the cameras or Gavin. Maybe by the little girl, maybe by myself, I don't know. It's a feeling I have. It makes me feel lonely – like someone is keeping their distance. They watch but they won't come close.'

'Do you feel like that all the time?' Lisa asked.

Kurt thought about this and realized that he didn't feel it right now as he talked to her. She waited for an answer, but he couldn't say it. Instead he smiled and shook his head and said, 'Let's steal some cake.'

Anonymous Male
Unit 300–380 Marks & Spencer

This is how we spend our Sundays now. It's become quite the tradition. Spend a few hours in bed reading the papers, and then we come down here. The papers always have something: a review of a book, or a CD, or a recipe. Even the bits that don't look like adverts are adverts really. They're not really newspapers, more like catalogues. Anyway, that's our mission for the day then. Go to Green Oaks and get that thing that we need. Maybe when we're here we'll find something else we want as well. Go home tonight, eat a nice meal, listen to the new album, read the first few pages of a good book – that's the weekend done. Always a little mission, then a little reward. We haven't found anything we want to buy today. We're going in all the right shops but nothing's really grabbing us. It's raining outside, though, so what else would we be doing? Sitting at home staring at each other. Going up the walls on a Sunday afternoon, that's what we used to do. Thank God for Sunday trading.

She's looking at the continental breads now and she's doing that thing with her face like she's saying, 'I'm quite profoundly unhappy underneath, and you are directly to blame, but I'm trying so hard to hide it.' She plays these games, like she's better than all this, like she finds our life empty or pointless in some way I wouldn't understand. I do understand of course. I understand everything about her, everything about us. I know her and she doesn't know me. I love her.

26

'My Heart Will Go On', on synthesized panpipes, seeped from the speakers. Kurt sat in the café in BHS waiting for his sister Loretta to turn up. His lap was burnt with hot tea that had flowed down the side of the teapot when he had poured. His elbow rested in a pool of UHT milk that had squirted out of the plastic pot when he opened it. He was eating a slice of cold, clammy apple pie that had cost £2.50 and the pastry felt like something dead in his mouth. His expectations were low, though, and shoddy reality couldn't break the luxurious promise of the words 'afternoon' and 'tea'. Like the eight or ten other lone customers in the café, he felt he was spoiling himself.

He and Lottie, as she preferred to be called, usually only met up once a year, an uncomfortable crossing of paths at their parents' house at some point over Christmas. Kurt knew his mother wished they could return to the closeness that bound them as children, but he didn't feel much about it one way or another. His sister had become estranged from the family when she was a teenager, and although in recent years, with the birth of her son, she had effected a reconciliation with her mother, she and Kurt had never really got back on track.

Kurt had been angry at Loretta's spectacular teen rebellion – partly because of the worry it caused their parents, partly because it was just so corny. He was disappointed that his older sister turned out to be so selfish and so silly. It was as if she'd read a manual on her fourteenth birthday and then went out to tick every checkbox in the clichéd repertoire of adolescent revolt. She became some sort of late-era postcard punk, ten years after the rest had all died out. She did the usual stuff with her hair, she pierced the usual places, she abused solvents, she stole from her mother's purse, she slept with every boy on the estate before moving out on her sixteenth birthday to live with a thirty-year-old man who called himself Spit. Kurt had met him only once. Spit turned up at the house one evening for Loretta, and their mother, desperate with worry and trying hard to do the right thing, insisted he came in for a cup of tea. Spit sat on the sofa and engaged in a silent twenty-minute stare-out with Kurt Sr while Pat kept up a constant stream of cheery banter, as if it was Joanie and Chachi sat in front of her on their way out for a burger, rather than Loretta and Spit out to burn each other with cigarettes. Eventually, unable to ignore the tremor in the left side of Kurt Sr's face, Pat desperately tried to engage Spit directly in conversation. She'd been glancing anxiously for some time at the white plastic bottle hanging from a chain around his neck. 'Spit, I must ask you about your necklace – what do you keep in the bottle?'

Without taking his eyes from Kurt Sr, he replied, 'Vomit.'

At which point Kurt Sr, as if he'd been anticipating the answer, shot out of his chair and thundered: 'Get out.'

Amazingly, Loretta and Spit (or Mark as he now called himself) were still together. They had married when Loretta was seventeen, they had jobs in IT, they kept lizards, they liked watching *Buffy* and *Deep Space Nine*, they tended towards cheap gothic in their clothing.

Kurt didn't know why Loretta had arranged this meeting. There was no ill will between them any more, but they were strangers with nothing to say to each other. To forge a relationship again would have felt too contrived and they both shied away from the awkwardness.

As Kurt finally noticed the feeling of wetness on his elbow, he saw Loretta coming towards him, watching him squeeze milk from his sleeve.

He poured her a cup of stewed tea and she got to the point.

'I thought I should let you know that Mom was attacked yesterday. She was walking along the High Street. Some glue sniffer tried to take her bag and she hung onto it. He knocked her to the ground – kept kicking till she let go. She wasn't going to tell us, of course. Didn't want to worry us. I called round last night to see if I could get her out to the cinema and I saw the state of her.'

Kurt thought of his mother's eyes blackened and his stomach turned.

'I wanted to see if you could try and talk to her, reason with her. She reckons this won't change her. She'll still carry on doing her shopping up there. "They won't get the better of me," she says – as if this is some game. Why does she shop in that war zone when she's got Green Oaks on her doorstep? It's ridiculous.'

Kurt stared into his tea, thinking about his mother, wishing he was with her now. 'She could come to Green Oaks if she wanted to. She doesn't out of respect for Dad. Green Oaks is an insult to him.'

Loretta seemed puzzled. 'Dad has no idea what's going on around him . . . and why would it be an insult? There was never any moral basis to his ban on us coming here.'

Kurt felt the usual irritation with Loretta's refusal to see things from anyone else's point of view. 'It's not logical, you can't rationalize it. It's a feeling – a sense of hurt. It's the way he feels and that affects the way Mom feels and how I feel. It makes me wonder if he's aware of what a disappointment I am to him, working here.'

Loretta looked at Kurt for a long time before she spoke. 'When I was fourteen, I came to Green Oaks. It had been open for a few months then, and I was old enough to find Dad's ban on it ridiculous, nonsensical. He ruled over us like some Victorian father, always the moral backbone of the estate, always quick to slap us down if we set a foot wrong. I was scared of him, but at fourteen I was starting to think for myself and I really couldn't see what harm coming here could do.

'So one day in the school holidays I just crossed the road and walked through the doors. I got here early to avoid any of the neighbours. It was dead quiet – just after opening. I couldn't believe all these shops, all this glamour suddenly on our doorstep. It was like a spaceship had landed over the road. I remember looking at this pink and white candy-striped jacket in the window of Clockhouse for ages – I wanted it so much. I thought if I had it, my whole life would change. I stared so long that my eyes lost focus and instead of looking at the jacket I was looking at the reflection, and that's when I saw Dad behind me. He had his back turned. He was wearing a cleaner's overall and mopping the floor.'

Kurt looked at her blankly.

'He worked here, Kurt. He was a cleaner here. There never was any factory job on the other side of Birmingham. When Green Oaks opened he got work here, like most of the women on the estate and a handful of men.'

Kurt couldn't take it in. It was impossible. 'Dad worked in Green Oaks? As a cleaner?'

'Yes, for years. And what's the big deal? Why the pretence? I mean what's the difference – factory skivvy, bank manager, cleaner, shit shoveller – what's there to be proud about? He had some very strange ideas about "real men", and "women's work" and all that stuff. I knew that at the time, but when you're fourteen you think you can change things. You think you can say "Don't feel like that" and it will work. I felt so sad for him. I just wanted to tell him that it didn't matter. Anyway –' Loretta shrugged '– he didn't see it like that. I remember he held my wrist so hard . . .' She trailed off, seemingly lost in the memory.

Kurt's head was full of questions. 'Why didn't you tell me?'

'Oh . . . he said he wouldn't stand for the family to laugh at him and that if I ever told you or Mom he'd walk out the door and never come back. Very melodramatic. I never did tell, but I started to see his misplaced pride as more and more ridiculous. I saw him as ridiculous and I set out to goad him. I'm thankful really: I was the lucky one. He stopped being someone to live up to, stopped casting a big shadow over me. I don't feel shit about myself or my life.'

Kurt said, 'Poor Mom –'

But Loretta interrupted. 'Don't worry about Mom. I suspect she found out a long time ago. Only someone as blind and stubborn as Dad would think he could keep it secret. I know she worries about you. She thinks you worship him, thinks you have to be protected. She tries to be the image you have of her as the devoted, brave wife – which is of course how she ends up getting mugged. She worries he has let you down, and you worry that you've let him down, and to me it's all a joke. You've been living in a dream, Kurt, and it's time to wake up.'

*

'Hello, Lisa, come in. I've asked Dave to spare you for a little while so that we can have this talk. As you know, I'm visiting the store today to touch base with the team and check we're all on the same page, but also I wanted to take this opportunity to speak with you.

'Now between you and me I know the Fortrell store is going to be advertising for a manager soon, and though I know Dave would be sorry to lose you, I think probably the time is right for you to maybe start thinking about the challenge of the future. I'm not going to say anything more about that right now, but what I will say is that it's vital if you're to move on and get a store of your own that you understand certain key concepts.

'Stop. I know what you're thinking: "But I'm duty manager now. What's so different about being store manager?"

'That's where you are completely wrong, completely. We are talking about different planets, different ways of seeing, and this is what I'm taking the time out to try and explain to you. Going forward you're going to be facing a whole new set of challenges, you're going to have to be driving a team in new directions. And you need to be in the right mental space in order to keep a firm grip on the wheel. It's a bit like putting on a new hat. Do you know what I mean by that?

'As you know, I do a lot of training for the company, and one of the first things a trainer has to learn is that you never blind your trainees with science. Too much jargon and you lose them. As a trainer, you have to remember that the people you're training don't know the first thing about the science of management. Doesn't necessarily mean they're stupid, doesn't mean they're not bright enough to understand . . . it's more . . . just ignorance. They maybe haven't thought about management before, they've just got on and done the job. They've muddled along blindly for God knows how long. So my point is, Lisa, I'm not assuming any prior knowledge here. I'm not going to baffle you with terms you don't understand and concepts you couldn't hope to get your head around in one day, right? What I'm going to do is walk you through two really important concepts, but I'm going to use what we call "mind pictures" to do this. Sorry – jargon! All mind pictures are, are a way of simplifying a complex message. They go back right to the start of history; Jesus used to use them in the Bible. In some ways Jesus was a manager too. A team leader. A fisher of men.

'OK, so the first one is what we call "The Ladder" and this is a way of helping you evaluate where you are and where you are going. So I want you to close your eyes for a minute and imagine a ladder. Have you got it? I should say, not an aluminium step ladder with four or six rungs – sorry, I should have made that clear before. I hope you don't have one of those in your head now, cos that's going to be a problem. What I mean is a big tall ladder, wood or metal, doesn't matter which. Now picture yourself on this ladder. You can't see the bottom and you can't see the top, but you're somewhere on the ladder. Below you, you can see Jim the team leader, and below him Matt, and then down and down until the last person you can see is perhaps some New Deal placement on the bottom rung. And then above you, just a few rungs up, is Dave, and above him Gordon, and you can just make out a few people above him but you don't recognize them, do you follow? So that is the mind picture that you and I have painted together. Now I'm going to leave that picture with you. I'm not going to try to interpret it for you. I want you to have a think about it over the next few days, this ladder, and when we talk next week, we might be talking about something completely different, maybe about footfall on level 3, and all of a sudden I'm going to turn to you and say, "Ladder," and you're going to tell me what you've made of that mind picture, OK?

'OK, good. You can open your eyes now. Lisa, open your eyes. Right, I'm going to draw something and I want you to tell me what you see, OK? Here you go, say what you see. Prawn? A prawn? As in Chinese take-away prawn? No, Lisa, it's not a prawn. I'll tell you what it is, it's a helicopter. Not a prawn at all. I want you to get used to the sight of this helicopter, because soon you will be getting in one of these every day. Now, don't get excited – the pay's not that great. Yes, you've got it: this is another type of mind picture. I don't know if you've ever been in a helicopter, but I have and I can tell you that from a helicopter you get a very different view of the world from down on the ground, can you see that? In your mini-copter you can swoop down on the shop floor, and from your altitude you can direct the troops in ways they can't fathom, bogged down as they are in ground-level detail. I want you to think about that.

'Phew. A lot for one day, right? You look like your head is done in. Let's go and make some customers happy.'

Mystery Shopper
West Car Park

Store code 359. Birmingham City Centre branch

Full report based on attached check sheets. I visited the store midweek at approximately 11.15 a.m. On entering the store a member of shop-floor staff was sighted within 60 seconds. The member of staff was talking to a customer. Three members of counter staff were at the tills serving a small queue. I milled around the main shop-floor area for 25 minutes but at no point was approached by any staff member offering to help me. Eventually I approached a member of staff and asked where I could find gentlemen's pullovers. The member of staff smiled and was polite but pointed in the direction of pullovers rather than accompanying me to the section. He also failed to ask me if there was anything else I needed help with. Raging fucking queen. After choosing a knitwear item I took it to the till. At the till the assistant failed to greet me and kept the transaction very brief. She did not ask me if I wanted the receipt in the bag. She did not thank me for shopping there. She did not express hope that she would see me again soon. Frigid bitch. Customer service score: 27%.

Restaurant code 177. A147 intersection Halesowen branch

Full report based on attached check sheets. I visited the restaurant at approximately 1.30 p.m. midweek. On entering the restaurant a smiling member of staff greeted and seated me within 17 seconds. The member of staff gave me a menu and assured me that she would return in 'a couple of minutes' to take my drinks order. 76 seconds later the same waitress returned and took my order for a double Scotch. At this stage she also checked if I was ready to order my food, or if I needed a few more minutes. I chose to order directly. The waitress told me about the day's specials in an informed and enthusiastic manner. I opted for a menu item and the waitress ensured I was fully appraised of all possible side dishes to accompany the main dish. She further ensured that her tits were in my face throughout this exchange. The waitress returned with the meal 7 minutes and 35 seconds later. She placed the meal correctly, offered me a wide range of condiments, smiled and instructed me to enjoy my meal. 2 minutes and 50 seconds later she returned to ask if everything was all right with the meal. I informed her that the meal was satisfactory but my cock was really aching and stiff, and requested that she take a look at it. A member of door security was at the table within 27 seconds and I was escorted off the premises in a further 15 seconds. No member of staff expressed hope that they would see me again. Customer service score: 95%.

Pub code 421. Quinton by-pass branch

Full report based on mislaid check sheets. Entered pub at 9.30-ish on a midweek night. Walked to bar and no fucker greeted, smiled or caught my eye for 11 minutes. Finally approached by fat unsmiling cunt. Took my order, and failed to inform me of range of pub snacks or ask if there was anything else he could get me. Sat at unwiped table with full ashtray surrounded by the ugliest creatures on God's earth. Undisguised additions to my pint from my hipflask went unnoticed by any member of staff. On second or perhaps third visit to bar, unsmiling cunt asked me whether I thought I'd had enough. At this point I carried out the toilet check on the gents. Toilets had last been checked half an hour before by staff member Tracey, but despite this I found them to be a far from inviting environment in which to vomit. In the absence of my usual working partner, the ungrateful bitch, I was forced to check the women's toilets also. Cigarette burns all over sink top fascia, my reflection looking scared through the vomit splashes. Two members of door staff helped me off the premises within 3 minutes. Informed staff and clients before I left that they had no fucking concept of customer service and that I fully intended to torch the premises. Customer service score: 0%.

27

When it came, it was a flat envelope, not a packet. She recognized her brother's handwriting, but could see that it wasn't a tape. She waited for a long time before she opened it, trying not to hope that it might contain a letter, words, a voice. She took a knife and cut it open.

Dear Lisa,

I find my voice is slightly cracked when I try and talk to you after all this time.

I wonder what you're like now. I wonder that a lot. Do you still have spiky hair? Do you still spend the hours between 9 and 11 a.m. worrying every individual hair with products and combs until they obey your will? I don't suppose so. Time moves on – or at least it should do.

I'm at home today, off sick. Had an accident at work last week and broke my foot. I'm looking out of the window at a beautiful blossom tree against a bright blue sky. I can't stop looking at it.

It's almost twenty years Lisa, did you know that?

I don't know what you think of me. I don't even know if you'll read this letter, or if you'll just throw it away. You must think I'm a coward, you probably think I'm something worse than that. I never stayed to find out. I still don't think I can face finding out now.

It's a long time since I seemed able to think of other people's feelings. I think I closed down at some point . . . I don't know, I remember feeling different in the past.

I seem to only ever think of myself – another reason for me to stay away – I'm not a very nice person, Lisa.

Are you married? Are you with someone you love? I hope so. I hope you're happy. I hope I never caused you unhappiness. I lived with a woman for a few years. A nice woman called Rachel. She was kind and she looked after me. She said she loved me. I said I loved her too. But I suppose I didn't convince her (I seem to have problems convincing people). We've split up now and I'm wondering how much the past is to blame.

I've been thinking about it more and more recently as I sit at the window and look out at the white flowers, the black branches and the blue sky. I remember at the time of the police interviews, when it was really bad and everyone's eyes said the same to me, I'd try and think 'In twenty years' time we'll all look back at this and laugh.' Well it's almost that now and I find myself thinking that again and again and wondering when I'm going to feel differently.

Some days I think maybe it's time for me to come back and face what I ran away from. Some mornings I wake up and think: this is the day I'll go home. But I always lose my nerve.

This letter isn't going anywhere is it? It's as directionless as I feel recently. I just wanted to write and tell you that I want to see you but I'm scared. For years I've tried to bury the past but it doesn't seem to have worked. I hope you don't hate me Lisa.

Love
Adrian

*

Kurt left the library and decided to walk the five or six miles back to his flat. It rained heavily the whole way but he wanted to feel the assault of it. When he reached home he lay on the floor of his living room still in his coat, filling the small room with the smell of outdoors and wetness. His sodden clothes made him shake. His mind raced.

Something in Loretta's story of her forbidden visit to Green Oaks had caused a long-buried memory to glow dimly in Kurt's head. He stayed in the café drinking cold, stewed tea for the rest of the afternoon, trying to work out what it was.

Whenever he had to try and dredge something from his memory, Kurt felt like he was playing one of those games of Hunt the Thimble when some annoying other would be telling you 'warm', 'getting warmer', 'oh, freezing cold now' as you tentatively probed the space around you. Once, when doing a crossword, he had forgotten the word 'peloton' and spent hours trying to find it in his head. Every time he ran a mental search he'd get a 'boiling hot' alert whenever he thought of the letter 'c'. When he finally recalled the word he was incredulous that it didn't start with 'c'. He was disgusted with his mind. Couldn't decide if it was malicious or inept.

So he knew there was rarely a eureka moment with memory. For him it was more like a slow, archaeological dig. Today in the café the memory had gradually emerged in all its unsettling and unpleasant detail. But even when he remembered it, he didn't connect the memory to his dreams of the girl on the monitor. It was only afterwards when checking the newspaper records in the library that he saw the photo once more and realized that Kate Meaney had come back to haunt his dreams.

As he lay on the bare floor memories flowed through his mind. He was back at the kitchen table of the house he grew up in, seeing her name for the first time.

He'd seen her in Green Oaks. He had noticed her trying to look inconspicuous, just like him. Trying to look like a child with a good reason for not being in school, a child with an adult. He'd seen the way she surreptitiously latched onto adults looking in shop windows, tagged along behind them carefully. Kurt had been impressed: she seemed practised at invisibility. He had felt every adult eye burning into him all morning. He was fleeing when he saw her, making steady progress towards the exit. This was his longed-for visit to Green Oaks, but he didn't like it – it was too bright, too risky. He was hurrying back to the factory plateaus, where he would be unseen. He had stopped when he'd seen her and watched her for a little while. He realized that she was invisible to adults because she was so preoccupied. She didn't look lost like Kurt, didn't look anxious; she looked intent, driven. A toy monkey stuck out from her bag and she was making notes in a little book, watching somebody in the distance. Kurt followed her eyes just in time to see the back of a man disappear through mirrored doors. She had glanced around and caught Kurt's eye. Her look was unreadable; it was saying something – an appeal or warning, but Kurt couldn't get it. He took it as a warning and left quickly.

The picture on the front page of the paper a few days later hadn't looked that much like her – she was more little-girlish in a dress – but he recognized the face. FEARS GROW FOR MISSING CHILD. His mother's back was turned, and so he carefully slid the newspaper alongside his comic. He carried on sinking his Sugar Puffs as he read it from the corner of his eye.

Kate Meaney last seen on Friday when she left her home to sit an entrance exam for the prestigious Redspoon School, but failed to turn up. A spokeswoman for Redspoon has confirmed that no paper had been submitted from the missing girl. Her grandmother, Mrs Ivy Logan, 77, widow, reported the child missing on Friday evening. Police conducted door-to-door enquiries and volunteers joined in the search around Kate's home and Redspoon, where the examination was held.

Kurt re-read that sentence a few times. Why were they looking there? Someone else must have seen her at Green Oaks. He couldn't be the only one.

Admitting to skipping school was not an option. Every other option seemed preferable to his father finding out not only of his truancy, but of being in Green Oaks. Kurt waited for a witness to come forward, someone somewhere to place her at Green Oaks that day. He tried to forget that he knew that only he saw her. He tried to forget the look that passed between them – the secret, silent language of children. The press coverage died down quickly. The girl didn't come from a normal family; she wasn't quite right for a tabloid crusade. Her disappearance troubled Kurt, it played on his mind, maybe not as much as it should, not as much certainly as the thought of his father's face if he ever found out he was skipping school for Green Oaks, but enough at times during that week to niggle him while he was watching *Superstars*, or playing British Bulldog. When he read on the eighth day that a neighbour of the girl had been taken in for questioning he convinced himself that he had been just about to come forward with the information, was just about to be brave, sacrifice himself and take the consequences, but now there was no need: a man was being questioned; everyone knew what that meant. And if no arrest ever came, and no body was ever found, maybe he never noticed. And in the months that followed maybe he just didn't connect the feeling that the house was watching him all the time with his little secret. He was fairly sure he was too young to realize what he'd done. Fairly sure there'd be no lasting consequences. Fairly sure his sleep would not be troubled by strange dreams for years to come.

28

The afternoon was a quiet time. After the lunchtime rush died down and before the final edition arrived there was time to re-stock, to sort through the newspaper returns, to worry if you had enough five-pound notes to last you until the next visit to the bank.

Sometimes a whole hour might pass without a customer. Mr Palmer kept himself busy. He was going to have to make some changes in his magazine ordering. No one was buying the old magazines any more. *Woman's Own* and *My Weekly* sat in the rack untouched. Cockney Dennis at the wholesalers had told him that men's magazines were the growth area.

Mr Palmer had looked at the covers and said, 'I've never stocked that kind of thing.'

'What do you mean?' said Dennis. '"That kind of thing"? These aren't like your *Fiesta*s and *Razzle*s. These are contemporary, a bit of fun, for lads.'

'I don't think my ladies would think they were fun. They come in to buy troach drops, herbal tablets, mint imperials – I wouldn't be able to serve them if that was staring up at us from the counter.'

Mr Palmer looked through the glass in the front door at the litter whipping in circles outside. It was always a sure sign of rain. He couldn't really care about the magazines today. He sat down and stared out at the swirling crisp packets. He couldn't care about much recently. He kept forgetting to take his lunch to work, or if he took it, he forgot to eat it. In the evenings he sat in the living room listening to the clock ticking and the occasional sound of his wife moving about in the other room. Loneliness was a physical ache. Jealousy was a sharper pain. She didn't need or want to talk to him any more; she talked to Jesus instead.

Last Wednesday he'd had a shock. There were four or five customers in the shop waiting to be served. He was turning round to get a packet of Lambert & Butler when he glimpsed the customer at the back of the queue. It was Adrian. His body was thicker and his hair was thinner, but it was his son. He looked straight into his eyes for a fraction of a second as he turned around to get the cigarettes. But even when his brain caught up and he realized what he'd seen, he didn't spin around to look again, he didn't shout his name. Time stretched. He stared at the cigarette packets. Adrian. He needed to collect his thoughts. He needed to say the right thing. He needed his face to send the right message. He lifted the packet off the shelf and turned back but his son had gone and the man held out his money for the fags.

Now the rain started and trickled down the door. He couldn't stop asking himself why he hadn't run after him. Why hadn't he thrown the cigarettes down, run out into the street, and chased after his son? Why hadn't he dragged him back? How had he stood there counting out the £4.56 offered to him and then gone onto sell some mints to the man behind while all the time his son was walking away? Instead he'd waited and waited, serving all but the last customer, before he'd said, 'Can you excuse me a minute?' and run out – too late – to the empty street. He stood outside looking frantically in all directions, and when he retreated back into the shop and felt the tears on his face he smiled at the man and said: 'It's a sharp wind all right today.'

*

It was cold and wet on the roof – but not in an altogether unpleasant way, at least not to Kurt. His clothes stuck to his body and the wind blew over his damp skin, but it didn't make him shiver at all tonight. He welcomed the harshness of the weather, feeling as if the rain was washing the sleep from his eyes. He leaned against the side rail and tilted his face, looking in vain for stars. Below him were acres of car parks, their rain-slashed emptiness lit every ten spaces by etiolated, spindly lamp posts. Beyond the car parks was the low-lying industrial estate, more darkly illumined but not silent, for even at this distance he could hear the rain bouncing off the metal roofs. Then there was the blackness of the scrappy scrubland that lay all around Green Oaks – the brownfield sites yet to be developed. The land was choked with weeds, littered with rusting extruded-metal offcuts from factories long gone, tangled with coils of wire and the occasional chunk of heavy plant machinery.

Kurt knew the scrubland well and yet all around it had changed as Green Oaks had spread and everything in the area had gradually turned its head to face the energy of the centre. When he drove about his old neighbourhood, he found that roads that were once busy were now cul-de-sacs, parks he had played in were cut through with new by-passes. The baffling complex of new roads sliced the area in unfamiliar ways and he was constantly surprised by old hidden places suddenly laid bare and open for everyone to see, while former key junctions were now silent, with grass poking up around dead-end bollards. On a clear day, from the roof of Green Oaks he could see the very top of the house he had grown up in – the house that he felt used to watch him when he was alone at night. Even now, through the sleet and blackness, he could feel it watching him still.

Kurt had thought about his father a lot since his

conversation with Loretta. He was trying to place him in a new context, running past memories to see how altered they seemed now. Tonight he thought back on a vivid scene from his childhood, the two of them standing together at a bus stop on a warm summer evening. His dad read the paper, and Kurt concentrated on willing the bus to emerge around the corner on the count of one hundred. Two boys were having a play fight behind them in the queue. They crap Kung Fued and lost their balance with every lop-sided high kick. They laughed louder and louder and swore at each other every time they missed. Kurt concentrated harder on the bus. Every time the boys swore he lost count. When they said 'fuck' for the first time he winced. He took a side glance at his dad, but he was hidden behind the paper. Kurt willed the bus to come. A bad word had unexpectedly leaked from the telly a few weeks ago. The word was 'shit'. Kurt Sr had put his paper down, walked to the TV, turned it off and told Kurt to go to his room. Worse words were flying around them now. A few of the women in the queue tutted at the boys. Kurt Sr read his paper. Kurt was nine. He was being taken to the cinema for his birthday. The boys were maybe thirteen. Kurt tried not to look at them. They were calling each other the c-word. The bus would not come.

Kurt Sr finished reading his paper, closed it and folded it into a tight roll, all the while watching the horizon for the bus. Then, without any change to his blank expression, he turned around slowly and, with considerable force, struck each boy in the face with the newspaper baton and said in his low voice, 'You and your filthy mouths belong in the gutter. Get away from my son and these ladies.' And they did, they ran before anyone could see their tears.

Kurt had never worked out whether he was embarrassed or proud of his father's actions that day and yet this memory had lodged in his mind. It seemed to capture the essence of who he had thought his father was: frightening, decisive, moral. He realized now that he'd been wrong to think he knew him, and foolish to let this assumed knowledge shape his own life.

The rain was heavier now, but Kurt was in no hurry to return to Gavin's toneless disquisitions on Green Oaks. It was as if Gavin knew exactly how inhumanly boring he was being and was just waiting for Kurt to challenge him. Just waiting for him to cut through the crap and get down to some other business. Gavin unnerved him.

He thought about Kate Meaney. He thought about his mind. He thought back to the first night he'd seen her on the monitor and wondered if it was his resolution to leave Green Oaks that triggered the dream. Maybe he thought it was time to move on, but the centre wasn't ready to let him go. And now he didn't know what he should do. Go to the police? Try and find her? Surely it was too late for these things. He wondered if he could have saved her – or would he have been too late even if he'd told his mother when he first saw the newspaper? He wondered if what he'd failed to do had actually made any difference at all.

His thoughts drifted to Lisa. He liked the way she looked at him. It made him feel like there was a point to him. Something about her made him want to say things, want to be open. He wanted to see her again.

Down below in the surface-level shoppers' car park, Kurt could see a handful of cars scattered about. There were always one or two cars stranded out here at night – maybe shoppers who'd stayed on for the nightlife and abandoned their cars for the evening, maybe people who'd forgotten they'd come in a car, or people who'd gone home in an ambulance instead – who knew?

Kurt had seen a light in the car in the far corner very briefly some time ago, but when he looked again he thought it was just the rain catching the windscreen. He decided to check it out anyway – maybe someone was sleeping in the car and that was not allowed. It would be a good ten-minute walk. Technically, according to Green Oaks' rules and regulations, what was not allowed was 'camping'. Kurt thought the windswept concrete plains would make unlikely holiday destinations, but Darren had explained that obviously what was meant was gyppos – tinkers, stinkers, travellers, paddies, pikeys, inbreds, dirty bastards and thieves of every shape and size – who'd move in, crap all over the car park and rob every shop as soon as you turned your back. Second in the rules after the coyly termed 'campers' were the 'joy riders'. No one was to have any joy in the darkened car parks of Green Oaks. Every safe, empty, commercial car park in the area was chained and barricaded each evening, forcing car thieves to hurtle murderously around the narrow roads of the nearby estates instead. The centre's regulations went on to prohibit any other 'clandestine presence' within the centre's borders.

Kurt was on the surface-level car park now and he walked slowly towards each of the three cars parked there. He found something very sad about a deserted car in an empty car park at night – it seemed to emphasize the loneliness and space. He shivered as he felt again that unmistakable feeling of being watched. He wondered if Gavin had the camera trained on him. As he started towards the old Fiesta in the corner, he thought he could perhaps make out through the rain someone in the driver's seat. He walked a little slower: he worried it might be a couple and he really didn't want to interrupt. It wasn't until he was within thirty feet of the car that he saw the tube leading from the exhaust to the stuffed up driver's window and he started running and stupidly calling out. He saw the man's flushed face inside and he knew he was dead, but he banged and banged at the window with his torch until he broke it and reached in and pulled the man's head towards him, and he was actually crying real tears for the first time in a long time, when his radio crackled and Gavin's flat voice said, 'That will be the third one since we opened in 1983.'

29

She'd been staring at the words for so long, they were bled of meaning. Hobbies and Interests. What did it mean? Technically it wasn't actually a question, and it was only the two inches of white space below that would clue you into the fact that the words were supposed to elicit a response. Maybe she could just write something equally ambiguous as a response: 'Good', or 'Hello', or 'Yes'. It was a conundrum. Obviously she had no hobbies and interests, she was a duty manager . . . and yet there were those blank two inches, as if they wanted or expected you to have a life outside of work. It was a trap, but the thing with these traps was to act as if you didn't realize it was a trap. Lisa knew that writing, for example, 'I find hobbies and interests take up valuable time that could be better spent developing top-notch merchandising skills in store' would be too obvious. She also knew that even if she had any interests, to list them honestly would be disastrous, a clear compromise of her commitment.

After twenty-three minutes of staring at the three words, she had a flash of inspiration and wrote: 'Shopping and reading magazines.' So simple. And true! They would be delighted that her life truly was that small.

She read back over the application form. She had her eyes screwed up the whole time, as if narrowing the aperture somehow protected her from the bad stuff bouncing off her retina. Fragments still embedded themselves in her brain. This was a signed declaration of abasement. Every shit-eating answer a direct plea for more shit. She imagined what Dan would say if he read this. Even his most florid, sucking on the corporate cock parodies paled next to the genuine article. She turned it face down on the table. She couldn't face thinking about Dan. He'd been so shocked when he discovered that Lisa was applying for a manager's job. The gap between his impression of Lisa and the person she'd become suddenly opened up and his massive disappointment shone through.

'I can't believe you're actually going to be a store manager. Hanging out with those gibbons at conference. Blackmailing seventeen-year-olds to work overtime for free. Making everyone around you work their arses off so you can get your bonus and buy a new car. I can't believe that's what you want. Don't you think it's bad enough here? You're going in completely the wrong direction. The way is out, not further in. You're going for the corniest piece of bait of all, the "designer loft". How vapid is that? How thin is that? "Living somewhere nice will make it all worthwhile." What are you talking about? Nothing makes spending twelve hours of every day doing something you hate worthwhile. I remember you when we worked together at Cyclops, you used to go to gigs, you used to enthuse about records, you used to do a lot of amazing photography. Do you remember that? Do you remember life before we spent every fucking evening shouting at each other about nothing in the Eagle? Do you remember our plans when we came and worked here? I said I'd do it for a year and then I'd travel. So it's taken two years, cos I buy too many opulent lunches, but I'm still going. What happened to the photography course you were raising cash for? How are you going to do that when you have a mortgage?

'First you drift into this weird, half-assed relationship with that fuck, and now under his influence you're doing this. I wouldn't care about you selling your soul, and living in your kit-built shitty designer loft, or even living with Satan's son, if I thought any of it was what you wanted, was actually going to make you happy, was in any way a consequence of your own volition . . . but I don't think that, I think you're sleepwalking. You're worse than the fucking customers.'

Lisa had said nothing for a long time, and then simply: 'I think maybe I am.'

And now as she sat at her kitchen table staring at the floor, she thought so again. Dan's words had all made sense to her, but had no real meaning. She felt a blunt, distant kind of pain that she had disappointed him. She knew she owed him more than that. He was the only person who really cared about what she did, but she was finding it impossible to get any perspective on her life. The episode had at least one positive outcome: it had galvanized Dan. The following day he quit his job and was now making preparations for his long-postponed travels.

Since she'd received Adrian's letter Lisa had felt increasingly dissociated from her everyday life. She knew she should stop and consider what she was doing, but she found herself unable to concentrate on anything except the possibility that Adrian might come back.

Having finished the application form, she made a concerted effort to think about Ed, about the flat they were supposed to be signing a contract for the following week, about the future, but largely she just recognized the recurring pattern in the carpet over and over and wondered if she should have a biscuit. The part she got stuck at was: 'What do I feel about Ed?' She found this impossible to answer.

She knew why Dan hated Ed; he told her often enough. Number one reason was that Ed was lazy, and though it was a fact that most people at Your Music hated their jobs, it was also a fact that they worked hard, largely because if you failed to work hard, someone else would have to do it for you. Whenever Lisa raised this with Ed, he made her feel like some corporate lackey, playing the manager. He'd say, 'I don't get paid enough to work hard,' which Lisa agreed with, but she also knew it was true of everyone. Ed would somehow turn his laziness and selfishness into a defiant gesture: if they all just did the minimum, things would change for the better at work. She always ended up hating herself in these discussions, hating the position she was forced to adopt and ultimately feeling she was wrong and Ed was right. At home it was the same. Ed would let her clean and tidy because he claimed he wasn't bothered by the squalor. He affected amusement at her middle-class desire for clean plates. As if such trifles were beneath him, as if he weren't middle-class.

Dan's more general reason for hating Ed was a wider contempt for the way in which Ed presented himself. He found Ed's way of drinking 'Scotch on the rocks' (and actually calling it that), his way of ostentatiously quoting Sinatra, his way of getting maudlin and self-pitying with his drink and hinting at some past darkness, his general attempts at a brooding noir persona . . . to be highly unimpressive. Dan would say, 'He's from Solihull for fuck's sake. What darkness does he have in his past?' And Lisa, who had orignally been slightly taken in by this noir persona, had been a little disappointed to find that indeed Ed had no dark past. Affluent parents, a pretty sister, three decent A Levels, but no darkness. Indeed his recent enthusiasm for loft living didn't seem very noir at all.

It occurred to her that she felt the same about Ed as she did about her job – a kind of numbed acceptance. She thought how rarely you saw the words 'numb' and 'acceptance' on Valentine cards, and thought how maybe she'd buy one for once if they widened their vocabulary a little. The words reminded her of her father in his brown cardigan with suede elbows. He had never offered Lisa any kind of fatherly advice or guidance, never urged her to keep up with her photography, never told her she was too good to be rotting in a shopping centre. He accepted every disappointment as if he had expected it all along, and he seemed to take some perverse enjoyment in being proved right. Lisa realized how like him she had become.

*

'. . . and that was the fifth one. The sixth was in 1995 and she hadn't even known she was expecting. I remember her cos she was young looking, I thought she was twelve or something, though they said she was sixteen. She had it in Celebrations Cards and Greetings, which at the time was in unit 47 but has since moved up to unit 231 and is now trading under the name "Happy Days". I was there when it came out of her. I saw it all. Her pockets were full of stolen gift ideas – like wind up birthday cakes, little plastic champagne-shaped bottles of bubbles, and a teddy bear with "Alan" written on its stomach. I'd been watching her all day. Turned out her cousin was the father, and I knew him cos I'd nicked him in the past, and when the baby came out it looked just like him and I thought I'll be seeing you soon, won't I? I'll be waiting for you. But of course I wouldn't cos it was dead, but I didn't realize at first. Stillborn and blue. The cousin was called Craig though, not Alan.

'Then there was a pause of I think three years, let me just check . . .'

Gavin glanced down at his notebook and flicked a couple of pages before continuing. The notebook was a new development. He had got it out from his locker the previous night to record details of the suicide. On the front was a slightly sloping Dymo-tape label which read: 'Green Oaks: Births, Deaths, Major Incidents'. He had interpreted Kurt's shudder when he saw this as a silent request to reveal the contents.

Kurt's head was drifting in and out of focus. If he drifted out too far he saw the man's face in the car, so he'd rapidly paddle back in again, back to Gavin and his little black book.

What was most unsettling, it dawned on Kurt, were the incidental details that Gavin included in each account, the details that no one could know: the thoughts of the glue sniffers as they fell from the roof, the last words spoken by the woman to her friend, the off-the-cuff present that the wife would never receive, the way the boy felt when the girl walked away, the waitress's true feelings about the obscene drunk, the voice in his head that wouldn't let him stay away, the funny feeling she'd had since she'd eaten the potato, the fear she'd smelled on the DJ's breath, the way the store was playing her favourite song when the baby was born, the way the paramedic's face reminded him of his father, the burning shame at having wet himself, the sudden memory of his wife's hair. Maybe Gavin made them all up. Maybe he made everything up. Maybe the notebook was blank.

Kurt drifted off. Grief stricken. The man had looked grief stricken. The face was an agony of loss as if leaving this life was too much to bear. And if he had gone over when he first saw the light maybe he could have talked to him, maybe he could have told him not to say goodbye yet. Perhaps he could have told him how he had wanted to say goodbye so many times after Nancy died, but he never did and look at him now, just look at him now . . .

'. . . he didn't die though. He broke almost everything, but not his head, which I think had been his aim. I think it was his head that was causing him the problems, but he fell awkwardly, or I suppose luckily you'd say normally, and so now all he wants to do is try again, but anyway that caused the gallery to be closed for three months and of course the Mulberry Tree tea shop was replaced in 1997 with . . .'

Nancy's face had been different, not grief stricken, not any emotion he could put a name to, because it just hadn't really looked like her, hadn't looked like any face she had ever pulled, so how could he attribute feelings to it? He hadn't broken down at the identification. They'd tried to tidy her up after the collision. There was some discoloration around the eyes, but there were no other visible wounds on the head or face. He identified her, knew it was her, but he felt no pain of recognition, no scream of finality. Finality came slowly.

'. . . but in that first year, no one died, no one was born, no one tried to kill themselves, no one saw ghosts, no one tried to blow us up, no one threatened to blow us up, no one glued up our locks, no one . . .'

Anonymous Male
Bench outside Next

OK, that's it.

Ten minutes now, fifteen at most. I've got to get out of here. If I don't get out of here I'm going to hit somebody, I can feel it building inside. I know the signs now. Fifteen minutes at most. She better be out by then. She knows what I'm like. I'm not supposed to get this wound up. She's the first to get hysterical when things go wrong but she's always putting me in these situations. I hate this place.

Why does she make me come here? She doesn't like coming on her own, says there was a mugging here once, so she wants me here to protect her. Sometimes she wants that, other times she screams if I tell some other bloke to back off. I don't want her mugged, so what can I do? She says 'You'll like it once you're there. You can go and look at the videos in Your Music.' Jesus Christ, I'd rather set my face alight than go in there. Have you seen it? It's like the end of the world in a pigpen. I can't stand crowds around me – she knows that.

I hate it here. I hate the way everyone looks at you. I hate the way everyone looks. There's a bloke sat over on the opposite bench who I would really like to hurt. He thinks he's something, but I could show him different. What would make him think he's anything?

This is a sick building. It's got that syndrome. It really gets to me. It's the smell or the lights or the music, I don't know. I always feel a migraine coming on – nausea, and then I get these feelings – which I can recognize now. I know they're not normal. I'm a sick man in a sick building. Recognition is the first step, but it's no bloody good unless I can get out of here quick. The music is doing my head in. M People for fuck's sake – it makes me want to crush somebody. I wish that bloke would piss off. I could go over there now and stamp on his head till he stopped smirking at every fucker who passes. I've seen him around the estate. He's nothing there, absolutely nothing. That is why this place is so fucked up, cos here he thinks he is something, and I really want to show him he is not.

She's got five minutes now, and then everyone is going to know about it, I think I'm losing control. God, look at the sight of that. Why are there so many fat bastards in here? They shouldn't be allowed out. It just makes me feel sick. Off to the food court to buy lard to squeeze in their tiny mouths on top of their balloon bodies. Fat, ugly or stupid – everybody. Look at their faces. Unbelievable. Like pigs in shit. God if I had a gun . . . But where the fuck is she? How many clothes is it possible to try on? Does she think I care what she wears? Maybe it's not for me. God, when I think of her sometimes in the British

Oak forcing herself in any bloke's face as she squeezes by to go to the Ladies. I sometimes think she's only with me to punish me. She's my sentence for all the bad things I've done.

Oh, Jesus, that fuck is chatting up some girl now – she's actually impressed by him – that's how wrong everything is. I'm shutting my eyes.

Please God, hurry up. I'm in real pain here.

30

Ed jumped up and down on the floor of the empty living room. When he was satisfied he lay down and put his ear to the veneer flooring. Now he started happily tapping on the walls. Lisa had no idea what he was doing. She was fairly sure he didn't either.

She felt ill. Everything in the apartment was brand new and the smell of plastics and dust reminded her of sitting in the back of her dad's car on hot summer afternoons as a kid. The sudden memory of heat-softened Opal Fruits made her want to vomit.

'All seems pretty sound to me, Lees,' said Ed.

Lisa stared at him. She had no idea where this was all coming from. She'd never seen him so animated.

He picked up the estate agent's details. 'I can't stop reading this: "A brand new luxury apartment in this exciting new development offers canal-side living within a few hundred yards of the Green Oaks business and shopping centre. Large master bedroom, with en-suite shower room. Fully fitted high specification kitchen leading onto living/dining area complete with balcony offering spectacular views over the waterfront."'

Lisa stood out on the small metal balcony looking down at a suitcase floating on the oily surface of the canal. It was unspeakably sinister.

'We could totally do this. Can you imagine living here? But we could. If you get the job at Fortrell it would be a breeze. Obviously, it'd be a bit of a commute for you, but then you said you didn't want to live right next to where you worked.'

Lisa tried to focus on the suitcase and not think about how it would feel living in the shadow of one shopping centre and spending two hours every day driving to work in another. The longer she looked down the more scared she became of the growing urge to throw herself off. She tried to fight the vertigo by looking out at the horizon. She could see the distant spire of the Friends Meeting House, its red Victorian brickwork marking it out from the grey blocks around it. She'd been in there once when she was six or seven. Her mom had taken her shopping in town. Lisa vividly remembered the orange skinny-rib poloneck she'd been wearing. She'd always liked it, but this day was the first day she'd worn it since a boy at school had said she looked like a tip-top. It was a stupid thing to say, and no one laughed, because she didn't look like a tip-top ('I don't think tip-tops wear jeans, Jason'), but she didn't really want to wear it any more. A woman with a clip-board came up to her mom and spoke to her.

Then she bent down. 'Hello, Lisa, your mom has said that you might be very kind and agree to answer some questions for us. It's nothing scary. It's not a test. We just want you to try a new dessert and tell us what you think.'

Her mom turned to her and said, 'It's market research, Lisa.' Lisa had no idea what this meant. She imagined trying to find something among stalls of fruit and veg and men shouting about polyester blouses.

The woman took them into a large room in the Friends Meeting House. Lots of long tables were laid out and here and there a child was sat spooning down some kind of coloured dessert. It looked like blancmange. They had blancmange at school and Lisa hated it. It occurred to her that her mother didn't realize this, because they never ate it at home.

Her mom felt her squeeze her hand and said, 'Aren't you lucky? A chance to eat all this lovely dessert.'

The woman returned to them carrying a small plastic bowl with some pink stuff in it. Lisa felt sweat on her forehead. She tried to keep calm. She'd had to eat things she didn't like before. Once she'd picked up a Jaffa Cake at her nan's house thinking it was a chocolate digestive. She'd had to pretend that she found the combination of stale sponge, bitter chocolate and orange jelly something other than foul, or at least until her nan turned her back and she could stuff the evil thing in her pocket. Now she had to be brave, she had to be polite.

'Go on then, Lisa, try some and tell us what you think.'

She put a small amount on the spoon and lifted it to her mouth. It was terrible, exactly the same as the stuff at school, but with the odd powdery lump. She swallowed the mouthful, took another quickly to get it over with, then pushed the bowl away.

'Nice,' she said with a wince. She reached out for the glass of water and drank half of it in one go.

'Is that all?' her mother said. 'Just nice?'

'Nice, thank you,' said Lisa.

'You liked that, did you?' the market researcher asked.

Lisa hesitated in case saying yes would mean more, but she could see the woman was taking the bowl away. 'Nice.'

'What mark would you give it out of ten?'

Lisa thought she should say a good mark: 'Eight.'

'Eight? That's good, isn't it?'

'Yes. Thank you,' Lisa said again.

The woman smiled and took the bowl away and Lisa started to stand up to go.

'Well, we'll see if that's the best of the five flavours then, won't we?'

It had been a terrible, endless afternoon. Gripping onto

the table edge as each new and somehow worse flavour emerged. Never deviating from 'Nice' and 'Eight', despite the mounting frustration of the market researcher. Going slower and slower despite the growing impatience of her mother to get home. She'd been polite, she'd done what she thought was expected and she'd got it all wrong.

She realized that Ed had been talking about the gym in the basement. She looked him in the eyes. 'I don't like it.'

'What, the gym?'

'The flat – I don't like it.'

'Well, Lisa, it's a bit late to –'

'Wait . . . there's something else. I don't love you, Ed, never have.' It was easier to say than she thought. 'And you don't love me, I'm not sure you even like me. What are we doing? Who are we pretending to?'

'How can you say that?'

'Because it's true, and if we don't say it now it will just get worse. You have to say right from the start or they just keep bringing you more bowls.'

*

Kurt watched Gavin pour 7-Up into a mug and place the mug in the microwave. Gavin hummed a little tune to himself. Kurt tried to read the paper. He had just endured a 35-minute presentation on Vestenburg Castle in Germany. Gavin had many photos of stone grey corridors quite similar to the ones he patrolled every day, albeit older and more worn. He said the castle had secrets like Green Oaks. Kurt had to get a tissue from his pocket at one point as he found himself literally bored to tears, something he'd never dreamt possible. The microwave pinged and he stared again as Gavin plunged a teabag into the boiling pop and, still humming the same non-tune, retrieved a clouded bottle of sterilized milk from his locker and poured in a generous splash. Kurt quickly looked away as Gavin made his way over to his favourite leather swivel chair, drank his tea with the bag still in, and stared fixedly at Kurt. This was something he did. Kurt had found that Gavin was unable to deliver his monologues unless he had eye contact, and so he had taken to keeping his head buried in the paper, or his notebook, or the back of a packet of Nice 'n' Spicy Nik Naks for as much of the time as he could. But Gavin, always the grandmaster in their unspoken gruelling encounters, had learned to counter this move by staring at Kurt's head, something he could always checkmate him with. Kurt had yet to develop a blocking move. He could tolerate Gavin's cold stare for two or three minutes max, before he felt the physical pressure of the gaze on his flesh. The printed words before him would start to slip about and, as he lifted his head to concede defeat and return Gavin's look, Gavin would begin once more.

'Do you often wonder what the future holds for Green Oaks?'

'Never,' Kurt replied without hesitation.

Gavin ignored him. 'This is Green Oaks Phase Five – and I think we all wonder where we go from here. I mean, where can we go? Phase One, of course, was the original shopping centre opened in 1983. Covering a now laughable 203,000 square feet, it was effectively just the north atrium. Market Place at the bottom, a few chainstores above. Lots of smoked glass and brown marble. Just six of us on security – easy money in those days. Kids were too scared to shoplift. They were used to High Street shops – nab the gear, step out the door and you're gone. Here though, step out the door and you're still inside. People used to think that electric shutters would come down on the outside when an alarm sounded – people thought it was some kind of space station. They probably thought we had guns – cameras everywhere – they were terrified.

We had an easy job for the first six months. The odd truant kid, but nothing like these days. No gangs, no knives, no violent head-cases. No mysterious sightings of little girls in camouflage jackets. It was my first job. I was proud of the uniform.'

At this Kurt snorted involuntarily. Gavin didn't react.

'Remember, Green Oaks took us in when others wouldn't. I'd been in a bit of trouble at school – and I'd paid for it many times over with my social worker, and my psychiatric visitor.'

Kurt winced. Gavin pronounced it 'psych-I-atric'. Just another little mannerism that made Kurt's flesh crawl. He hated these allusions to Gavin's past. He knew he was expected to ask what he'd done, and he knew if he did, he'd get some finger-on-nose 'less-said-mate' crap. Gavin was just like the other bullshitting security guards in that respect – trying to play up their bad-lad pasts.

'March 12th 1986, the dawning of a new era. Green Oaks Phase Two is born – perhaps the most ambitious phase. The first brick is laid for the three new malls. Totally different design – using, of course, C E Glaistow as the contractors this time, not McMillan and Askey after the problems with the ventilation in the service corridors. Glass roofing, mirrored walls, chrome finish – an altogether airier feel inspired by the Müller Einkaufszentrum in Germany. No one likes the north atrium now; even with a refit it still seems brown and old. I remember when they put in the glass lifts – direct from the States – you couldn't get the kids out of them. You must have started a few years after this. Did you have any idea just how state-of-the-art the security facilities were? Everything top spec. Did you realize how lucky you were?'

'I felt blessed,' said Kurt from behind his hands.

'And now we're up to Phase Five – all the canal-side development – Wharf Edge. Total lifestyle concept – shop, live, play. Course if you work here you can't afford to live here . . . we commute in and they commute out. It's *Upstairs Downstairs* all over again. Mrs Bridges the cook, Gavin the security guard, Asif the cleaner, Sayeed the stockroom boy – they keep us all busy.'

Gavin paused and looked at Kurt's closed eyes. 'You don't like the dead ends, do you?'

Kurt was suddenly alert. 'What?'

'The dead ends. The cul-de-sacs. The service corridors that lead nowhere. You don't like them. I've seen you sometimes on the monitor. You won't turn your back on them. You – what? – that's it, you retreat . . . backwards, until you reach the turn-off, then you turn and carry on your way. Now, why would you walk backwards unless you were scared to turn your back? What's there to be scared of?'

'You fucking watching me, for one thing.'

'You don't want to be scared of me.'

'Don't I?'

'No, mate, I'm nothing to be scared of. Those walls though . . . you know you should be grateful: there's less of those cul-de-sacs now than there used to be. They get bricked up, once they're sure that the corridor won't be needed, that nothing's going to be developed that will need servicing, they seal them up. So behind some of these walls we walk along are pockets of dead air. Little chambers of nothingness. But you knew that already.'

Kurt looked away. 'Maybe I heard it before. You might find this hard to believe, but I don't retain that kind of detail.'

Gavin fixed him with his pinhole stare. 'You're right. I do find that hard to believe.'

31

Lisa saw Martin from across the shop floor. She was about to relieve him of his stint in the Classical Department, where Ian the buyer was off for the day. Martin was standing not behind the counter, but at the glass doors of the department, eyes flicking nervously across the outer shop floor searching desperately for his replacement. He looked like a dog waiting to be let out – it was a genuinely pitiful sight. As she opened the door he scooted past her before she had time to step over the threshold. Lisa sighed and made her way to the counter. At least there were no customers.

Sealed off behind its glass doors, with fake walnut walls, leather armchairs and soft music playing, the department gave the impression of a refuge. Somewhere to soothe the jangled nerves after a day spent on the singles counter. It was, however, a false impression. The truth was that the Classical Department was hell in a box.

The other departments attracted the odd eccentric, the occasional trying customer, but Classical drew the elite like some powerful catnip emitting its scent across the city. The truly obsessive, the disturbingly odd, the terrifyingly pedantic – they all flocked to the glass box. Lisa imagined one day setting a valve on the door that let the customers in but not out, and then when the department was full, pouring in pectin and setting the customers in a kind of rich jam.

She started clearing the chaos behind the counter. Every now and again, under the piles and piles of seemingly orderless Deutsche Grammaphon CDs and copies of *Private Eye*, she'd find an empty bottle. It went unremarked that Ian was an alcoholic. A bottle of whisky, a vast knowledge of classical recordings, a corrosive line in sarcasm and an impressively explosive temper were the only ways to get through the day in the glass box. Ian's retirement, which at the age of fifty-eight was approaching fast, was something no one dared to think about.

As she placed the composers in alphabetical order, she worried about her dad.

Now Ed had moved out she found herself finally starting to do some of the things on her list. She had made a rare visit to her parents the previous Sunday and was angry with herself for leaving it so long. She didn't worry about her mother. She had spent the entire visit talking to Lisa about articles she had read in smudgily photocopied pamphlets about the End Times. But there was a sadness in her dad's face when Lisa left that had made her feel bad. She'd always blamed her father a little for Adrian's disappearance, but recently she'd started to question why. She'd thought her father had been complacent, that he should have convinced Adrian that he had support. But now she wondered what he could really have done. What could she have done? The letter she'd received from Adrian had made her realize that it was Adrian's decision to leave, and it would be his decision if he ever came back. Her dad wasn't responsible. She thought of him at home with her mom and her pamphlets and wondered if he ever got lonely. She decided to call in on her way home and see if he might like to go out for a drink.

She was trying to think of somewhere nice to take him when she heard the unmistakable announcement of Mr Wake's arrival in the department. Mr Wake got about in an electric wheelchair which he was unable to drive. His arrival was invariably accompanied by cheery whistling and the sound of CD units collapsing as he crashed into them.

'Morning, Lisa. How are we today?'

'OK, thanks. How are you, Mr Wake?'

'Well you know . . . I'm surviving. So, Lisa, I believe you should have had another delivery today – any joy yet?'

It was unbelievable that Mr Wake could still be waiting for the tape he'd had on order for twenty-three months. But as he unfolded the tissue-thin, torn and scuffed special order form, Lisa saw that he was still optimistically expecting Mozart's *Horn Concertos* on cassette to turn up one day. She cursed Ian under her breath. It was of course never coming, had long been deleted. She'd tried to tell him that the tapes were being phased out – everything was on CD – but it made no difference. Mr Wake had read it was available and so he visited three times every week to check if it had arrived, each time with the same initially high level of optimism, followed swiftly by the same heart-breaking disappointment. Ian loved it. He never tired of making a big pantomime, searching through boxes, pretending he'd sighted it earlier that day – always finishing with a smile and 'Oh well, Mr Wake – maybe tomorrow. I'm sure it can't take much longer.' He delighted in torture. On one particularly foul-tempered day he went so far as to tell Mr Wake that it had come in the day before but had been sold by mistake. Lisa just didn't have the heart or strength to tell Mr Wake one more time that she was sorry.

He was a tiny man with a particularly tiny head, as if the scale had been shifted slightly above his shoulders, and yet today, as if to emphasize his shrunken cranium, he had chosen to wear a large deerstalker. Lisa had been so absorbed in his tragic special order slip that she only now noticed with a start that on his hat was pinned an open bus pass. She realized that this was probably to free up his hands to try and better control his unruly electric chariot when getting on and off the bus. It was an ingenious solution to this problem.

As soon as she saw it was a bus pass, Lisa knew that she should on no account look at the photograph. The photograph she knew would have an effect. The photograph was not to be glanced at, because even a glance might provoke a response she wasn't able to control. The bus pass was catching the light, but Lisa was keeping her eyeline steady on Mr Wake's sub-hat-peak face. The peak was the plumb line; if she saw that crossing her field of view, then she should look away, because after that she would see the photo, and that could not be.

All went well for a couple of minutes as she was able to check the computer screen for the inevitable non-arrival of the tape. But when she turned back Mr Wake coughed, causing him to lower his head more rapidly than Lisa had been prepared for. She should have dragged her eyes away, but it was too late, she had seen the photo. She stared at it, unable to blink.

The bulk was taken up with the curtained rear wall of the photo booth. But in the bottom left-hand corner, huddled in at the edge of the frame, was Mr Wake. He seemed to be cringing as if facing a firing squad, trying to shoulder his way through the hard plastic siding of the booth to escape the bullets. His tiny head tilted tremulously up at the camera from his bunched shoulders, and his eyes were wide with horror. He was trying to avoid the light from the flash, shrinking backwards to evacuate space for the light to fill. But the flash had reached him, as was evidenced by the look of terror on his face. Above his face was a retaliatory flash back at the camera, where the gleam from the white explosion was reflected in the opened bus pass on his hat. And on the bus pass was another, presumably older photo, which Lisa could not see clearly, but imagined contained a similar shot, and perhaps it was the recursiveness, this endless series of ever-diminishing Mr Wakes that led something inside her to break.

She was paralysed for some time staring at the image. Eventually she heard Mr Wake calling her name and she shook herself.

'Lisa, Lisa, are you all right? Is there any joy? Has it come?'

Lisa stared at Mr Wake again, and then without speaking she walked over to the CD section and picked up Mozart's *Horn Concertos Nos. 1–4*, went to the accessories for a blank sixty-minute cassette, returned to the counter, put them both in the stereo and said: 'You'll have it in ten minutes.'

It was time to get out.

Anonymous Female
Sainsbury's Car Park

Sundays are the worst day. And every Sunday is worse than the last. I sit in the empty house all day. I move from room to room, from one chair to another. I think I might want a cup of tea and turn the kettle on. Then I realize I don't and I turn it off. I think I might need something from the corner shop, but I can't think what it might be. I look out of different windows and see all the other windows in the street, but no one else is looking out. I never see another face. I wonder what they do on Sundays. I stand there looking through net curtains, at other net curtains and time moves very slowly.

I thought I'd come to the shopping centre. It's something people do on a Sunday. I've seen them passing on the buses. I knew there'd be hustle and bustle here. It's hard not to have a purpose in this place. I went to Sainsbury's. I let a large woman untangle her trolley before I attempted to get one. Everyone else pushed past me and grabbed trolleys, but I waited for the woman, I didn't want to push past. Eventually she got her trolley and walked straight into me. She didn't seem to see me. She ran over my toe.

I've been stood here for quite a long time now. I don't seem to be able to move. I know I'm in the way, I can hear people tut. Maybe I should ask for help, but I'm sure if I spoke no one would hear.

Sometimes I think it would be better if I didn't exist, but then on Sundays I'm not sure that I do anyway.

It was a mistake to come here. Another mistake. I'm tired of them, really.

32

Lisa wasn't able to visit her dad that evening. Two officers were waiting for her as she left work and had taken her straight to the police station. It hadn't taken long. She was back home before dark. The flat was cold when she got in. With Ed gone there was no one to leave the heating on all day every day. She was hungry, but the thought of cooking or even entering the kitchen seemed impossible. Instead she sat in the living room in the fading daylight. The dusk drained everything of colour and left only shadows and outlines. She sat completely still and felt herself become part of the room – nothing more than a shape. She thought she might stay like that for ever.

She looked at the dark outline of the phone for a long time before she picked it up. The first two attempts at dialling the number didn't work. First she got an engaged tone, next a seemingly bewildered woman who kept shouting 'Kaz?' into Lisa's ear until she hung up. It would be easier if her hands stopped shaking. She dialled a third time and after a couple of rings Kurt answered the phone.

'Hello, Mom,' he said.

Lisa was thrown by this and when she tried to talk she realized she hadn't spoken for hours and her voice had become a croak: '. . .'

'Mom? I've been trying to call you –'

'It's me, Kurt. Lisa.'

'Oh – hello.' There was a pause. 'Well, now you know that my mom is the only person who ever phones me.'

She didn't react to this. 'I got your phone number from your boss. I hope you don't mind.'

'No, it's good to hear from you. How are you?'

Lisa didn't answer, she didn't know how to. She thought it wasn't too late to back out of this, there was no rational reason for going ahead, but instead she said, 'I have to see you.'

*

He was relieved to see no evidence of a boyfriend. The flat smelled and looked like it had been scrubbed only recently. Lisa looked tired when she opened the door and as the evening went on Kurt noticed that she seemed less chirpy than she had on their previous meetings. He thought it might be the drink. He had taken round a bottle of Dalwhinnie and they'd been hitting it quite hard despite Lisa's original concern that she'd be ill. Kurt had brought it to kill his nerves: he couldn't remember the last time he'd sat and had a drink with anyone. He couldn't remember a time when he'd wanted to. He'd yet to find out what it was that Lisa called him to say – though it was obviously something beyond the superficial chat about films and music that had passed so far. The only thing that linked them was the girl – maybe Lisa had discovered something. Slowly the conversation became less neutral and more personal and, as it got late, they sat drinking whisky, telling each other stories of the past.

*

1 A.M. – KURT

'There used to be an old guy who played guitar around the town. I suppose he was a busker, but he never laid his hat on the ground and he never got any money. He didn't have a regular pitch. I'd come across him unexpectedly in some doorway or by the church or at the bus stop. He was an incredibly slow guitar player – incredibly. It would take him seconds to change the positions of his fingers between notes. But he never played simple, slow tunes that might have suited a slower hand; his repertoire was always very intricate, technically difficult guitar pieces, slowed down so much that you needed to stand still for maybe five or ten minutes before you realized what the tune was. It was as if he didn't want to leave a note until its every nuance and possibility had been fully explored. And I would stand, often for an hour or more, listening. I wasn't really interested in the tune, instead I liked to get lost in each note, each one a work in itself. And the man's face wasn't a face twisted with effort or frustration as he forced his fingers into the right shape, it was a face of bliss, real transcendent, unselfconscious bliss. I found the whole performance just beautiful, though I think he was as unaware of my appreciation as he was of everyone else's derision.

'One cold day I saw him up by the old cinema. He was playing some endless convoluted arpeggio. He was wearing a balaclava with no hole for the mouth and in front of him on the ground was a white card which said: "Alphonso in concert. Playing live tonight. Black Horse 9 p.m." I never knew till then what his name was.

'There was one other person at Alphonso's performance. A woman with dark red hair who danced throughout the whole two-hour set, which I think was actually just one song. I sat at a small table with a candle, and across from me was the only other table and chair, as if he had known only two of us would turn up. At the end of the song Alphonso shook his head a little and seemed to notice us for the first time. There was a moment of embarrassment in which I didn't know whether I should just leave, or thank him, or carry on sitting until he left the stage. The woman remained on the other side of the room and we continued to act as if we hadn't noticed each other.

Then Alphonso spoke as if to a large crowd: "I'd like to dedicate this next song to the two young lovers here this evening," and then launched into an old Django Reinhardt standard that he played with breathtaking fluidity and deftness, zipping along through the finger-knotting gypsy jazz and singing in a beautiful delicate voice.

'What could we do? We went and got drunk together. She was called Nancy. We spent every night for the next five years together. We never saw or heard Alphonso again.'

2 A.M. – LISA

'I've been thinking recently that my brain is a bit broken. I don't think it's doing what brains should do. I noticed it a few weeks ago while I was waiting for the computer to churn out the day's figures. I'd been staring at the wall for maybe ten minutes, when I realized that all I'd been thinking in those ten minutes were thoughts almost too minute to document – thoughts along the lines of "wall", "pinboard", "grey", "paper", "patch of brown" – not really thoughts at all, just basic recognition functions. So I tried hard to think about my thoughts in general and I realized I really very rarely had any, any more. Not just thoughts, but enthusiasms or feelings or ambitions or anything. I'm not sure how long this has been going on for. I set off every morning on the drive to work thinking I'll chew over some issue in my head, and maybe I'll get as far as phrasing the central question, but within minutes it's just "traffic lights", "blue car", "grey sky". I don't seem to have any crazy synaptic diversions, or any level of abstraction that makes me better than a . . . snail. It reminds me of maths lessons. I was crap at maths. Whenever I'd try and concentrate on some concept my mind would go blank, just completely and literally blank. Time would pass, papers would be collected. I was in the bottom stream for five years and that was exactly the right name for it. Everything was murky and submerged down in the bottom stream. But the thing is, that blankness used to be remarkable, it was only true when I had to think about vectors or differentiation. Now the blankness has spread.

'And I was having this realization the other day. I was also remembering how when I was a child I was unstoppable. I remember the way I was always busy, always on a mission, always scouting out something or other . . . usually music. My brother was a lot older than me but he couldn't see a reason why a little girl shouldn't be fully aware of every step in Lee Scratch Perry's career, or the exact point at which David Bowie became shit for ever, or why Johnny Cash was great and the Doors a joke, or why Bob Dylan was the enemy. He used to make these compilations for me and they'd contain a few deliberately duff tracks to test my critical faculties. I mean I was eight at this stage – he turned me into a monster. At first I'd just say I liked everything on the tape, but after a little while I started to identify the lame tracks, and in the end he used to laugh cos I'd launch into these ridiculously intricate and stinging assaults on tracks he actually liked and I'd even convince him sometimes that the track was in fact derivative or contrived or a pale shadow of earlier work. When you're that age I think music can penetrate you more than it ever does again. I would get lost in the landscape of an album or a single, it would just close around me. I'd get the bus into town and go to the old Virgin store and spend hours reading the books in there, looking for clues and pointers, earnestly reading lyrics, searching for signs. My brother would take me to gigs – we must have been an odd sight, he was twenty-two and I was thirteen – but they were the best days really, the best days of my life. I don't think I'll ever feel as focused, or as engaged in anything as I did when we used to go and see bands. I seem to have lost all that now and I miss it. Now I work twelve-hour days and my brain is broken and I don't seem to hear music at all.'

3 A.M. – KURT

'I was grieving before she died. For three months before the car made impact. Sometimes I think that the car was getting closer that whole time, slowly picking up speed, accelerating to make my loss complete. One day you wake up and everything is different . . . that really can happen. It really can happen that in the night when you are both sleeping, curled up tight in each other's arms, something changes for ever. I could sense it in the shape of her back when I woke up, something about the aspect seemed unfamiliar, angular, changed. It was her birthday and I reached under the bed and pulled all the presents out and placed them around her. I wanted her to wake up surrounded by parcels, and so I placed them delicately on the sun-warmed quilt even though there was something about the way she was lying that made me think she was already awake. But I whispered her name and she didn't respond. The sun was bright on the bed and she'd wake up in a few minutes. We always woke up within minutes of each other. But she didn't stir. I thought about the order in which I'd have her unwrap the gifts, saving the best till last. I think an hour passed and then suddenly she just turned over, and her eyes were open and I knew she'd been awake the whole time, maybe for hours, turned away from me, staring at the wall, and of course she knew I knew. And it was as swift and as brutal as that. She didn't love me any more. She never said anything. I think she was as shocked as I was. She kept going through the old motions, saying she loved me, maybe hoping it would come back. Neither of us said anything. Sometimes at night I couldn't help myself and I'd cry and cry and cry, and she'd hold me in her arms, neither of us saying it, and I'd burrow deep into her arms, forcing my body closer and closer, squeezing harder, trying to feel that old certainty, that completeness, and there was nothing there.

'Three months of that. I wonder how long it would have gone on for before she had to leave. How long would I have carried on having little lapses and forgetting that she didn't love me any more? How long before I stopped needing the reminders? After three months the car deleted her completely, and then suddenly my grief was legitimate and not shameful, tragic not trite. And at the funeral everyone said to me, "She loved you so much, you know, you were everything to her, everything," and I'd nod and say, "I was, I know, I was. It was perfect."

'So I buried it, buried it as deep as I could with sleep and dreams, thinking maybe I dreamt those last few months, maybe it was love until the end. I thought maybe it was impossible for something so real and so big to vanish for ever, I tried to lie to myself . . . but you know the truth now, and you have to remember it for me. It's hard for me to remember sometimes, I mean it's a hard thing to remember, but I don't want you to let me forget. You'll hold my hand like you're doing now, you'll hold it with your ice-cold hand and I'll know it was true, and I won't sleep through it next time.'

4 A.M. – LISA

'I was supposed to be meeting my brother in Wimpy at eight o'clock. We used to go into town together, but that night he had some other business to attend to first and so he left the house early. My dad drove me into town. I was thirteen and he didn't like the idea of me getting the bus at night on my own. Wimpy was safe, though – what bad thing can happen under the gaze of the Beefeater? I was sitting there drinking my fizzy orange drink, looking at the tickets for about the hundredth time. We were going to see Kraftwerk . . . and it was just like science fiction to me. I was past excited – almost sick, really – I couldn't believe we were going to see them, in the flesh, or circuitry or whatever they were. Kraftwerk were a place in my head, an atmosphere, a certain feeling. The idea that Kraftwerk actually existed somewhere out there, and even weirder, that other people in this city also knew of them and listened to them was just amazing to me . . . it kind of appalled me. So I looked out of the window and tried to guess which of the people walking by were going to see them, but it was beyond me. These were people with shopping and umbrellas and woollen overcoats, people with brown curly hair and bicycle clips, people with carrier bags. These worlds were not commensurate. My mind ached at the improbability of it all, or maybe at the anticipation – as desperate to see the audience as I was to see Kraftwerk. And it really was a slow and awful torture that night to see the clock hands ticking by and my brother just never materializing. I only had the money for the one drink, not even enough for a phone call. There's a certain combination of orange pop with the taste of plastic cartons that instantly brings back that feeling of hopelessness and panic and disappointment. Every few minutes I would resolve to just go on my own, but then I'd imagine my brother running up to the plate-glass window searching for me and I couldn't do it. It's funny: he never did run up to the window, but I have that image planted in my head as if it happened. I can see the look of panic and apology on his face. In the end though it was my dad who came and collected me.

'My brother had been detained at the police station. A little girl called Kate Meaney had gone missing near where my brother worked, and it seemed my brother was the prime suspect, though he was never charged. No one was ever charged, a body was never found. In the weeks that followed, the police questioned me about my brother, about our "relationship" – what does that mean? We were related . . . so what? They asked me horrible things. They kept saying I must feel lucky to have a brother who paid such attention to me, but they didn't mean that, I could tell that even then. They didn't have a clue about music. I came back from the police station wanting to tell him all the crap they had said, I wanted to tell him how one of them had written Kraftwerk on his pad as Craft Work, how they'd got excited when I mentioned us getting the *NME* together cos they thought I meant the enemy – how mad is that? But my brother could barely talk to me, he wouldn't look me in the eye. He couldn't bear what they might have made me think, and I should have told him explicitly: they didn't make me think anything, but I thought it was obvious – to state that would be to imply doubt, and doubt never crossed my mind. Nothing changed for me, but he didn't trust anyone any more. I know it was hard with the abuse from the neighbours, and Dad tight-lipped and Mom weeping all the fucking time, but I was there, his compadre, and it was as if I was invisible to him.

'He moved away. I think at first he thought he'd go until the girl turned up again, or until someone confessed, but of course that never happened, and so he never came back. I haven't seen him in twenty years. He disappeared just like the girl. I still wonder how he could do that. How could he have so little faith? Not enough faith to even look in my eyes. How could he repay true faith with desertion?'

*

It was 5 a.m. Through the window the sky had turned from black to blue and the birds still found something to say about that. Kurt couldn't look at Lisa. He felt sick.

Whisky mixed with shame and horror. Did she know? Did she realize it was his silence that had kept her brother under suspicion? His head spun.

Lisa was tired but clear-headed. She thought now was the time to say what she wanted to say. 'You found a suicide in the car park last week, didn't you?'

Kurt nodded, keeping his eyes on the floor.

She felt the tears drop from her face onto her lap, but she waited until her voice was steady before she spoke.

'I had a visit from the police. It seems you found my brother Adrian.'

Kurt pushed back the chair and fled.

Anonymous Youth
Sainsbury's Rooftop

The centre gates are locked at night but it's easy to get in. We walk into the car park by the UCI as if we're going to see a film, but then we walk right past the cinema and across the car parks to the shopping centre. You just cut through a few hedges – it's not hard. We know where the cameras are: it's just guards we have to look out for. I got caught by one of their dogs when I was seven, and it ripped my leg open. I carry a knife now and I'd stab one in the throat if it came near me again. Jason is scared of dogs, though, and we wind him up by telling him there's an alsatian in the shadows, and he laughs and tells us to fuck off, but he breaks into a little run anyway.

I remember on that day that Tracey wrote some shit in the lift going up to the roof. Some stuff about her and Mark 4 EVA, and she asked me what the date was so she could write it underneath, and I looked at my watch to tell her, but when I looked back Mark was kissing her. Anyway that's how I remember it was twenty past seven.

Summer Sundays are the best cos we don't have to wait

till dark. The staff are all gone by about half six. We got to the roof and it was like afternoon, and Rob ran to each edge and looked over to see if there was any sign of guards or dogs. Jason got out the glue and we laughed cos he'd nicked so much. And Craig got out his lighter fluid, cos he doesn't like glue.

I don't know how long we were lying there for. I was watching a cloud that looked like a tank roll across the sky. There's no building taller than us, no one looking down on us. Then Jason came running over with the trolley he'd found left out by the lift. We all had goes bombing it over the roof. Then Rob said let's all try and fit in. So Mark and Tracey scrunched up in the basket part, and Craig and Jason sat on the edge, and Rob lay over the top with his head facing forward, like the little dog thing on the front of Jaguar cars. There was no room for me, so Jason goes, 'Give us a push, Steve.' So I started pushing them about. I could see Tracey's face pressed up against the mesh inside and she was laughing and I remembered how it was when I used to go out with her. I had a headache from the sun and the glue and it was knackering pushing them about, but I felt OK cos I was remembering the time Tracey used to kiss me. She said we were 4 EVA but it was only six weeks. I was running with the trolley and I suddenly felt stupid pushing them about, felt stupid hanging about with Tracey now she was with Mark, felt stupid that I was on the outside and they were on the inside, so I stopped. But I suppose all the weight meant the trolley carried on further than I thought, and I tried to call them cos it was going faster and faster down the slope, but they were laughing too hard. I could see the front wheels about to hit the edge and I was screaming, and as it tipped, everything became a photograph. Mark and Tracey were still in the trolley but now it was upside down, Rob was still horizontal lying motionless in the air, and Craig and Jason both had their hands in the air like there was something to hold on to. They all stayed like that till the photo in my head was developed, and then they vanished.

33

The house was spotless, she was sure of that. Every day she hoovered and mopped and dusted, but once a week she did a big clean. A spring clean – except it was weekly. Curtains down and washed, inside the oven scrubbed, behind the fridge de-crumbed, condiment sets emptied, washed and refilled. It took a good seven hours and now she sat at the teak-effect dining table with a *Puzzler* magazine in front of her. The house smelled of Windolene and she watched the nets and sheets blowing wildly on the line in the garden. It made her feel so free to see them fly and billow: she could almost feel the wind ripping through her, blowing her away.

She went into the kitchen and made herself a cup of tea the way she liked it. She still revelled in being able to do that. She put the second spoon of sugar in and nobody frowned. She cut herself a generous slice of the coffee cake she'd made the previous evening. She was going to sit down, eat her cake, drink her tea and answer questions about celebrities. No one was going to make her feel bad. The house was silent. He was sat in his usual chair facing the front window. She stayed in the back of the lounge at the table out of his range of vision. She was perfectly happy.

When Kurt Sr first had his brain haemorrhage it had been a struggle. She'd needed Kurt at home to help her manage – feeding him, changing him, washing him, getting used to that stare. But as time went on it became easier and it wasn't long before she realized how much happier she was with him as he was. For years she'd been like a bird, flitting about him nervously, trying to do the right thing but never seeming to please. Now the chill of his disapproval was gone and she could do what she wanted – even if that was only as daring as putting sugar in her tea or buying the odd magazine.

It was true that she still never shopped at Green Oaks, but that had nothing to do with him. Of course she knew he'd lied about his job. A neighbour had spotted him at Green Oaks soon after he started there, but she had more sense than to let him know that she knew. She just didn't like it there, couldn't understand why anyone would want to shop in a place like that. Couldn't understand why everyone flocked there and deserted the local shops where people knew your name and asked after your family. The attack had shaken her, but it wouldn't stop her.

She washed her cup and plate and looked at her reflection in the kitchen window. Just like Gregory Peck, that's what she'd thought the first time she saw him. He was tall and dark and sombre. When they first started courting she cast him as a romantic hero. She thought the severe exterior masked deep passions. She thought that on their wedding night she would be the key to unlock him. She knew how proud and happy she would be to have this serious figure entirely devoted to her, besotted by her. But she had been wrong. The severe exterior masked nothing but more severity and joylessness. On their wedding night he behaved as if following a manual. He barely seemed to notice her as he pushed and manoeuvred mechanically. Afterwards his only comment was that he didn't know what all the fuss was about.

They'd fallen into a pattern where she spent her days trying desperately to please him, and he spent his never being pleased. She thought maybe children would change him, but the children soon learned to creep around him too. Kurt stammered as a child and Loretta used to hide under the table. She couldn't help feeling elated when Loretta rebelled. When other mothers would have buried their heads in shame at their daughter's conduct, Pat felt nothing but pride. She worried about Kurt, though: he was too like her, too worried about his father's approval, wasting his life trying for something that didn't exist.

As often seemed to happen, she was thinking about Kurt when the doorbell rang and there he was stood in front of her, looking like his father did all those years ago.

'Hello, love, I was just thinking about you.'

Kurt stared. 'Oh, Mom, look at your face. Why didn't you tell me this had happened?'

'What would you have done? Except worry. What's the point in telling people bad things?'

It could be the family motto, Kurt thought. He looked at his father – he'd seen him through the curtainless window staring out with his fierce eyes.

'How's he today?'

'Oh, the usual. Bit of a performance at breakfast this morning.'

'How are you?'

'I'm very good, son, very good. Don't worry about the bruises, they'll fade. I'm not scared of some kids. I know their names, I've told the police. I'm not scared of them at all.'

Kurt smiled. 'You're Joe the Lion, made of iron, aren't you?'

'And what are you made of? Sawdust and glue it looks like. What's the matter with you? You look terrible. Are you eating right? Are you sleeping at all?'

'I'm OK, Mom. I haven't been sleeping recently, but it's OK.'

'I worry about you, you know.'

'I know.'

'I love you.'

'I know, Mom.'

'You'd tell me if something was wrong, wouldn't you?'

'What's the point in telling people bad things?' Kurt replied – mimicking his mother's voice.

She laughed. 'I've got to pop out to the post office before it closes to pick up his money. Will you stop for your tea?'

'Yeah, I'll see you in a minute.'

Pat went out and shut the door and Kurt pulled up a chair in front of his father. He looked into his eyes for a long time, longer than he could usually stand. Then he started to speak, in a quiet voice.

'She's better than you deserve, better than you ever deserved. Did you hear what she said? Nothing stops her. She's made of iron . . . and what are we made of?

'Can't sleep at the moment, Dad. Not a wink. I lie awake and I look at the car lights as they move across the ceiling. I've been thinking about the way I am and what made me that way. I've been thinking about you too.

'Do you know that you never spoke to me when I was growing up. You told me what to do and what not to do. You issued instructions. I don't think that makes you a good father. I don't think you turned me into a good or a strong man. Well, just look at me – I'm a sack of shit.

'I saw Loretta the other day. She told me about your secret life as a cleaner – I had to laugh. I can't believe you lied all that time. You lied and you hid the truth and for no reason. I don't hate you for that. I hate you for passing on that weakness to me. For giving me your weak genes. I hid a truth for years, hid it so deep that I almost forgot it. Forgot to think about the harm that might have caused. I was always more worried about disappointing you.

'I watch the orange lights fly across the ceiling and wonder if I should tell her. "What's the point in telling people bad things?" I say to myself. "It's not going to bring her brother back." But that's not what I'm really thinking. I'm really thinking how I like her, and she makes me happy and I'm too weak and selfish to lose that. Better to stay quiet.

'I'm just like you, Dad. A liar and a coward. Does that make you proud?'

34

In a room smelling of candy-foam sweets, Lisa looked at the display boards. Gavin had been given some forgotten old unit in a stagnant tributary of the centre to stage his 'Green Oaks 21st Birthday' exhibition. She was due to meet Kurt at the fountain at six. He had phoned her and said he wanted to talk to her. She wanted to talk to him too. She wanted to tell him that she'd quit her job, to tell him he should too, to tell him how she felt. And now, killing time before she met Kurt, she found herself at Gavin's exhibition, which seemed a fittingly dismal way to say farewell to Green Oaks for ever.

She'd already said goodbye to Dan. She met up with him before he left the country and told him that he'd been right about everything: the job, the flat, Ed. He laughed when she told him how she'd quit on the very day that Gordon Turner finally made his long-threatened store visit. She'd given him the guided tour, making sure he saw the blocked fire exits and the boxes of stock hidden in the ladies toilets – where, as an added bonus, they also came across Graham the stockroom boy, who'd been instructed by Crawford to hide for the duration of the visit. Dan told Lisa that he'd done a lot of research and had worked out the countries to avoid on his travels in order to eliminate all possibility of returning home with dreadlocks, stripy trousers or any kind of ethnic jewellery. He said he was steering clear of the entire Pacific rim just to be on the safe side. He promised her that he would never swim with dolphins.

The unit where the exhibition was had once been a fancy sweet shop, where you could buy landfill candy at fifteen times normal shop price and they'd put it in a glossy pink striped bag for you – but the only people who had visited the dimly lit cul-de-sac were those who were lost and they never wanted to pay 25p for a coconut mushroom, they were looking for the toilets. Lisa felt something soft underfoot and saw an old candy shrimp had stuck to her shoe. She decided she'd leave it and see how much confectionery her shoes accreted for the time she was in there. She liked the idea of walking around on a mangled wreckage of Flumps and Flying Saucers.

Gavin was sat in the corner having taken holiday leave in order to invigilate the collection. Kurt had warned Lisa about him, so she wore a Walkman to protect herself from commentary as she looked at the endless photos and blueprints. She knew that to stand in front of any item for too long would be an invitation for Gavin to come and talk. She listened to Smog and the sound of Bill Callahan's bitter despair went well with the bleak images.

Her brother's death gave a new angle on grief for Lisa to try and gauge. She was learning that there were different degrees to loss – subtle gradations invisible to most. Loss through suicide had a different grain to loss through vanishing. She wanted to talk to someone about it. She wanted to talk to Kurt. She didn't know why he'd suddenly left her flat the other night. She felt as if she was starting over, as if she was awake for the first time in years. Despite everything, she felt a hard, burning, bright light inside her whenever she was with Kurt, and now as she hummed quietly along with Bill's baritone, it seemed to be the first time in a long time she'd heard music.

She moved from photo to photo. Some were official publicity shots, others were clearly from Gavin's own archive. She moved onto a particularly dull section consisting of photographs of the service corridors. She noticed that the rear areas had originally been even bleaker, with the doors and pipes unpainted. She thought it typical that the staff passageways were left unfinished for some time after the centre opened for business. Gavin's childish block capital captions spelled out even the tiniest details: WHILST THE SHOPPING AREA HAS HAD 17 REFITS TO DATE, THE SERVICE AREAS WERE PAINTED JUST ONCE IN 1984. A man in white overalls painted a corridor grey. Lisa thought of the grey paint on the back of the monkey she'd found. She was shocked to realize that the monkey must have been there for twenty years waiting for someone to find it. As she looked at the photos she felt a growing sense of revulsion towards Green Oaks. Image after image captured endless facets of its malevolence. An ambulance-man held a traumatized child in his arms outside some kind of Christmas grotto. The Lady Mayoress, in powder-blue trouser suit, cut the ribbon on the second mall. Police tape on the roof where some glue sniffers had fallen off. An eight-foot Bugs Bunny with his arms around dead-eyed children outside the Warner Brothers store. A distant shot of a blurred figure inside the lift. Keith Chegwin, thumbs aloft, surrounded by workers dressed as dustbins. A grainy shot, probably a CCTV freeze-frame, of Kurt walking across a dark car park.

She wanted to be outside in the light. She wanted to leave now and never come back. She turned to flee and didn't even notice that Gavin had gone too.

35

Kurt noticed that along the bottom of all the buildings in the street were faded stains where dogs had pissed. He was glad he didn't normally notice that. Someone passed by with a dog on a lead straining to sniff some fresh stain, and Kurt wondered if the dog ever looked up and noticed the buildings above the stains.

He sat in a café opposite the police station drinking tea, postponing going in.

It was two days since he had met Lisa and told her about having seen Kate the day she disappeared. He didn't decide to do it: the light changed and the words came out. He had phoned her and asked to meet her. They were walking through the woods in Sutton Park when the sun came out from behind a cloud and shadows appeared all over the forest floor. Kurt stopped and kissed Lisa. He told her he loved her. He told her that he wanted to always be with her and then he told her he was responsible for her brother's death. He felt a strange mixture of euphoria and terror. They sat on a pile of logs. He held her hand but she looked away. He watched the shadows of the branches move over her skin.

Eventually she spoke. 'So she was seen after Adrian left her. If you'd told the truth Adrian would have been eliminated as a suspect, rather than living under a cloud. He'd probably be alive.' She brushed an ant from her arm. 'I don't know what to say. I can't find any anger. I don't know why. I wish I could really. I listened to you and then

I waited to see what feelings came, but there's no anger. I don't know if it's because you were a child. Or if I just can't imagine any other past. Or because, after what you said when you kissed me, I don't want to imagine any other future. I feel sad. I wish we'd known this a month ago. I wish we'd known twenty years ago. But I knew this would happen one day – proof would come. It doesn't seem to change anything for me.'

Kurt watched the ants march over his trainer. 'I want to go to the police. It might do some good.'

Lisa sighed. 'You can go if you want, but I wouldn't expect a warm reception. They're quite attached to their current theory.'

Now he sat in a white room thinking how right she was. It wasn't like on the telly. No one offered him tea. No one sat with a tape recorder. He'd waited for ages for a detective to speak to him and when one finally arrived he'd seemed busy and distracted. After a while he'd stopped seeming bored and became unpleasant and insinuating instead.

'So, you're belatedly reporting a sighting of Kate Meaney on the day of her disappearance?'

'That's right.'

'And you say this monkey is evidence that she was in Green Oaks.'

'Yeah, it was found there, in the service corridors.'

'And how do we know this monkey has anything to do with Kate Meaney?'

'Because I remember seeing her with it on that day.'

'And the monkey was found by Lisa Palmer, sister of a suspect in this case?'

'Yes.'

'And Lisa Palmer is your friend?'

'Yes.'

'And we all like to help our friends, don't we?'

'What help is it? Her brother's dead. I'm not lying.'

'Look, the death of her brother, it brings it all back, doesn't it? Gets a mention in the papers again. Of course she doesn't want that hanging over her for ever. I don't suppose you do either.'

'Do you always treat witnesses like this?'

'I always check that my time's not being wasted.'

'I'm not wasting your time. Take the monkey, run tests on it, check it for fibres, check it for fingerprints, carbon date it . . . I don't know what you do, but you must be able to find out if I'm lying.'

'Oh, we can find out.'

They stared each other in the eyes until the detective abruptly stood up.

'Wait here. I'll get some forms to fill out.'

The door slammed behind him and Kurt banged his head hard on the table. He hated himself for keeping quiet this long. He hated the fact that he'd help furnish the ugly minds of the investigators. Most of all he hated what he'd done to Lisa.

The detective returned looking more pissed off. 'Well, Kurt, I'm afraid you're going to have to wait here a little longer. We're truly blessed today. It seems the Detective Chief Inspector has heard about your claims – God alone knows how. She's on her way. She wants to talk to you.'

1984

STAYING IN THE CITY

36

'How long has it been now?'

Kate looked at her watch. It was the one her father had bought her the last Christmas before he died. It was digital. It had twenty-four functions. The time glowed red on black right through the night. Kate thought it was perfect for nocturnal stake-outs.

'Twenty-seven minutes.'

Adrian sighed. 'The 966. We should have known. Take my advice, Kate: don't ever catch a bus with a number higher than two hundred.'

'Why not?'

'Because they run about twice a day. Because they go to places that no one wants to go to. Places where weird people live. They go to the countryside, Kate.'

Kate wrinkled her nose. 'I don't think I like the countryside.'

'You'd be mad to. It's brown and it's depressing. Muddy fields. Grey skies. Pinch-faced people. Pylons.'

Kate thought for a while. 'I think axe murderers live in the countryside too. I think I've read that somewhere – maybe in my book.'

'I think that's probably right. Axe murderers. Gun owners. Hat wearers. Cows. It's a terrible place. And do you know what else? They don't have shops.'

Kate thought for a moment and then said, 'They must have some shops. How do they get things?'

'No, they don't have shops. They have these things

called Spars. They look like shops but they don't sell anything except maybe some swede and a packet of custard creams. The owners pull a gun on you if you ask for anything else.'

'I don't think that's true,' said Kate.

Adrian didn't bother to respond, he'd depressed himself too much. He rubbed his hands to keep warm.

Kate looked again at her watch. What if she was late for the exam? Or missed it entirely? That would solve all her problems. But she'd told her grandmother she'd go, and she didn't break promises. Today was a Friday and the exam was going to take up the entire morning. Kate burned with anxiety. She was currently spending every weekday evening and all day Saturdays waiting for or watching her suspect. Very exciting developments had passed in the last week – she knew the time was drawing close. She'd decided not to return to school after the exam. She'd say that she'd missed the bus. She had to go to Green Oaks. That morning she'd left home in her dad's old camouflage jacket. She realized that the camouflage wasn't designed for blending in with shopping centres but she needed the pockets for her camera, tape recorder, notebook and many pens. Mickey was safe by her side in her canvas bag. Adrian had insisted on coming with her when he heard she was going to make the three-bus journey on her own. Kate would normally protest at any suggestion that she wasn't fully independent, but she was glad of the company. She drew the line, however, at him waiting for her while she did the exam. She wanted to get straight to Green Oaks afterwards and that was classified information for only Mickey and her. She insisted to Adrian that she could get back to school fine by herself.

After a further fifteen minutes the bus finally crawled into view. Adrian and Kate chose the front seat upstairs but the larger view from the seat only served to dismay them. Kate looked out as the city thinned out and gradually slid into dismal brown fields. She knew that she was missing vital pieces of evidence while she sat and endured travel sickness on the endless bus ride. She imagined living in a school. She imagined living away from shops and streets and blocks of flats. She imagined living away from Adrian and Teresa. She closed her eyes to keep the tears inside, and after a while fell asleep against Adrian. She dreamt about the suspect. She was following him down a corridor. He was carrying a big sack, but money was falling out and every time Kate bent down to pick it up, the banknotes turned into pages from her notebook. She was scrambling around trying to collect all her evidence and the suspect was escaping. Suddenly she felt something tugging at her and woke up to see Adrian standing up and gently pulling her arm.

'Come on, Kate. This is it.'

37

Adrian said goodbye at the bottom of the drive. In fact he didn't say goodbye, he said, 'Keep fighting, sister. Remember – the revolution will not be televised.'

Kate had no idea what that meant, but took it as some kind of farewell. She smiled weakly and walked through the gates. As she trudged up the long drive in the rain, the outline of the gothic school grew larger and more oppressive. Cars passed by and splashed her, seemingly unaware of her existence. In the car park Kate hesitated and stood sheltering under a bike shed. She watched as estate cars and Range Rovers pulled up. Agitated parents flapped as they ushered their children towards the school hall and a golden future. Kate looked at the other girls in their pastel pinks and their bobbles, and felt like a different species. Couldn't they have got the bus on their own? She looked at their empty faces and saw the answer. She thought for the seventeenth time that morning of running away, but she had made a promise. Well, she'd been made to make a promise, and she couldn't break that.

Kate entered the hall to a scene of chaos. Strident, confident voices of parents clashed in the warped acoustics of the wooden-floored school hall. The children stood looking constipated on the sidelines as the parents marched around furiously trying to find their names on the desks. Kate walked over to the first row of desks and saw that the names were arranged in alphabetical order. She walked a deliberately circuitous and slow route towards the M's.

Cund, Duck, De'Ath, Earwaker, Onions, Spammond. She imagined having to sit through register every morning surrounded by these extra-terrestrials. Her thoughts were interrupted when she finally got to the desks of Mauld and Mongah and found no Meaney in between.

All around the small invigilator, parents pushed in front of Kate and shouted for attention.

'My daughter doesn't have a pencil.'

'It's O'Nions not Onions.'

'She must have a toilet break every hour, you must remind her, she won't say herself.'

'Where can I wait?'

Eventually, moments before the paper was due to start, Kate spoke to the examinations officer. 'I can't find my desk.'

'Have you looked?'

'Yes, that's how I know I can't find it. My name is Meaney, but the desks go from Mauld to Mongah.'

'Yes, well, you're not the only one.'

'Oh, OK.' Kate could see that the woman was giving her about five per cent of her attention.

'Yes, something has gone very wrong with the registration this year and Mrs Breville will have to answer for this. We have a list of schools who are submitting candidates, but not the names of the candidates, which would be more helpful I think, don't you? What school are you from?'

'St Joseph's.'

The woman looked down her list. 'Yes, we have one candidate listed from St Joseph's.'

'OK.'

'Yes.'

There was a pause, then Kate said, 'So where shall I sit?'

'Yes, well, you will have to do as the other girls have, which is sit on the far row, and fill out a registration form now. This will be stapled to your exam paper.'

Kate walked slowly over to the final row. The room had emptied of parents now, and as she made her way to the only remaining empty desk, the other girls all concentrated fiercely on filling in their names.

She did not want to go to Redspoon. She thought of watching some dreary game of hockey on muddy fields while Tamara Onions tried to find her pencil. She imagined seeing the headlines about the multi-million pound robbery at Green Oaks. She remembered her promise to her grandmother to do her best and she felt sick. After seeing the other girls she was surer than ever that doing her best would guarantee her a place at the school. She picked up her pen to fill in the registration document. Submitting School. Candidate Name. Home Address. And then as she wrote the name St Joseph's, it all became clear to her. The solution had been obvious right from the start. She would not break her promise, she would not go to Redspoon, she would do right by everybody. Next to Candidate Name she wrote in clear capitals: TERESA STANTON.

2004

THE LOOKOUT

38

One time she woke in the middle of the night to find Kate sat at the end of her bed looking at the dressing table with a puzzled expression. Teresa could almost reach out and touch her, but instead she woke her husband to see if he could see her. He couldn't, of course.

He sat up in his ridiculous silk pyjamas and said. 'You don't believe in ghosts, do you?'

It was more evidence that they were all wrong together. She'd been gathering it for some time.

She didn't believe in ghosts. They believed in her.

Kate was always with her. She sat behind her when she was caught in a tailback on the ring road. She was somewhere to her left, just outside the beam of the desk light, when she read reports. She was the smell of sharpened pencils that Teresa noticed when she was tired. Kate believed in her.

She let her head fall back on the rear seat headrest and looked up at the city as it slid over the surface of the car. Shapes and lights flew past the windows: lit squares in dark office blocks, people spilling from bars, abandoned cranes, clocks that had stopped. She saw these things and they passed straight through her. She didn't have to think about them or process them. She wanted always to be a passenger.

The car descended into the Queensway and the grime-encrusted lights in the tunnel reflected fleetingly in her eyes until they slowly closed. She thought of the man found pink-faced in his car. She couldn't bear to look in the mirror any more. The truth could have saved him, but the truth wasn't a friend of hers, it hadn't got her to where she was now.

She had always known that Adrian Palmer's version of events was true.

The detectives who worked the case thought he was their man. They thought the case was closed. She'd looked at the files a hundred times and each time she got itchier at their sloppiness, their incompetence, their assumptions. They'd let Kate fall through the net and Teresa had to mask her fury and contempt every time she saw those same detectives at the coffee machine or swaggering along the corridor in their slip-on shoes.

Of course she'd always had an advantage over them, evidence that they didn't possess, evidence she chose to withhold. She knew that Kate had sat the Redspoon exam.

The car followed the big dipper of Birmingham's ring road, swooping down into tunnels and then up over flyovers. Teresa was tired but buzzing – wired for the interview ahead.

Once upon a time there was a girl with bruises, a girl who ate scraps, a girl who didn't know the rules.

Kate had given that girl an opportunity and she had taken it with both hands, running and running with it until there was no one else around her. After public school came university and then her career with the police. Journalists would come and interview her. She was a story. The colour of her skin. Her gender. Her rank. They found this combination endlessly interesting. She was an inspiration, a shining light. No one on the force had results like DCI Stanton, but the journalists never asked about the one result that mattered – that remained hidden. They would ask what drove her – but she would never say ghosts. They would ask what made her – but she would never say secrets. They would ask who – but she would never say Kate. Instead it was dull PR with local hacks in bad leather jackets. Teresa thought she could save them all a lot of time and column inches if she told the truth. It was a one-line story: she had one aim, one goal, one debt to repay – she was going to find her.

But she'd never had a break. She'd researched, she'd questioned, she'd squeezed informers, but no one had seen her: Kate was the invisible girl. Teresa had been following the trail to the same dead end for twenty years. Kate put down her pen at the end of the exam and vanished into thin air.

Until today. Teresa had been tipped off. A man had walked into a police station carrying a stuffed monkey. He'd been hiding the truth for all that time and Teresa really couldn't hate him for that. The driver waited for the barrier to the station car park to lift and Teresa felt a rush of adrenalin, knowing that the truth was coming. Kate was coming to the surface.

39

The investigation focused on staff working at Green Oaks at the time of Kate's disappearance. Kurt's new eye-witness account had Kate following somebody into the service corridors, so staff records were trawled, names run through the criminal database, doors knocked on. One luckless pair of officers were sent to interview Kurt Sr and found the experience just as unrewarding as Pat had told them it would be.

Gavin's name stood out from early on. He had a string of juvenile offences, too long in the past to have prevented him working as a security guard at the centre. As a teenager he went through a phase of breaking into houses. He never stole or caused criminal damage: he just liked being in other people's houses, liked looking around. More significantly, he also had an unauthorized absence from work the day after Kate's disappearance.

When Teresa saw him, the hairs stood up on the back of her neck, as they always did when she knew. Before she questioned him she watched the video he had made of the service corridors. She took the tape home with her and watched it in her apartment. The shaky camera moved through the grey corridors. Sometimes Gavin's breathing was audible, sometimes he'd provide a snippet of commentary but mainly it was just the sound of his footsteps on the hard floor. Teresa found herself sucked into the screen. The images stopped looking like concrete corridors and instead she felt herself being pulled through some vast organism. The footsteps seemed to be hers and she had no control over where they took her.

She was still staring glassily at the TV after the footage had ended and static filled the screen. Thoughts of when she and Kate had been ten filled her head. It seemed to her now that back then they had burned like the sun – so much light and energy that nothing or no one would be able to extinguish them. She watched absently as shapes emerged from the fuzzy grey screen and she realized that she was the one who had faded, the one who had been fading for years. Like a star, Kate might have died a long time ago but her flickering light still reached Teresa, still guided her.

She was lost in thought for maybe twenty minutes when the static on the screen turned to rolling lines and a picture broke through the snow. It was the service corridors again – some unidentifiable corner – but this time Gavin was in front of the camera. He lay on the concrete floor, the side of his face pressed to the ground, his eyes open and staring ahead. Teresa watched with tears in her eyes and knew she'd found Kate.

40

'I'd felt her eyes on me before. I wasn't used to that. I spent my life watching other people. No one ever watched me.

'I'd sense a gaze on my back and I knew she was there sitting somewhere behind me. I didn't know who she was or what she wanted, but I knew she'd chosen me.

'I never seemed to think quite in step with other people. Even when I was a kid – always at odds with everyone else. It made life difficult at school.

Surveillance is a case in point. You hear people talk about "victims" of stalking, or they talk of the hunter and the prey. I don't see it like that. When you watch someone, you have no control over where they go. They can do what they want and all you can do is stand in the shadows and watch. It's a feeling of powerlessness. But when someone's watching you, you're in charge. If you move, they move. Have you ever been watched like that? Do you know how it feels?

'She seemed to always be there. I'd sit by the play area watching the children. I used to watch them for hours – no one seemed to mind. After a short while I'd feel her eyes upon me. I felt myself being closely observed, my movements noted, no longer invisible. She started following me around the centre. I'd catch glimpses of her in shop windows and mirrors. It seemed like my power over her grew gradually. Each day she'd follow me more closely and for longer. Then one day she followed me through the mirrored doors into the service corridors.'

There was a long pause, but Teresa kept silent and waited for him to continue.

'I didn't have any idea of where I was walking. I had no thoughts, just the feeling of pulling her along by a string through the twists and turns of the corridors. I could hear her footsteps behind me. I never turned around – that would break the spell. I didn't want it to end.

'I walked out of the fire exit on the upper west side and still she followed me. She hesitated at the exit, and there was a terrible moment when I thought it was over, but I think now she was leaving her toy behind, the one the girl found. I should have noticed it, but I never did.

'I don't suppose you know, but back then the whole area on that side was a building site. It was land earmarked for expansion of the centre, but the development had barely started. It was difficult land to build on. Some parts of land had to be excavated for foundations, others had to be filled in to raise the level. Work had stopped altogether because the centre wasn't proving to be as successful as first hoped, and the owners were getting cold feet about the costs of further development.

'It felt strange to be outdoors and still know she was behind me. There was nothing for her to hide behind out there, nowhere for her to go. If I turned around I'd see her, but I didn't want to do that. I wanted to keep going and always have her behind me. I dropped down the sides of the development, until I reached the foundation level. The ground was very slippy and uneven but she kept coming. She had no choice.

'The foundation area was vast and in the middle of it were some lower plateaus that would have to be raised up. I dropped down onto one of these and I remember there was a sheet of wood and some stones arranged on the ground. Something drew me to it and when I got there I moved the wood with my foot and saw it was covering an even lower level – some sub, sub-basement of the old factory. A ladder was fixed to the side of a narrow shaft and led down to darkness. I think I wanted to be in the dark, I think I wanted to know if I could still feel her eyes in the black, but maybe that's me thinking that now. At the time, I'm not sure I was really thinking. It was as if we were both programmed – her to follow, me to lead. I don't think I had a choice.

'I climbed down the ladder and stumbled about a bit until I found a wall. I sat down against it and waited for her to come down. I liked the idea that I'd be able to watch her descending the ladder, but I'd be invisible to her.

'I heard her footsteps approach the entrance. I knew she'd come down, the bond between us was unbreakable. I watched her right foot slowly move over the edge and onto the ladder and then the other one reached over for the next rung. But somehow the left foot missed. I see that image in my mind a lot. The foot trying to step onto something in mid-air. There was a brief moment where I saw her clearly as she fell through the shaft of light and then she disappeared into the blackness below her.

'There was something about the sound she made when she hit the ground that meant I knew she was dead. I went to her. I sat down beside her. There was a little light where she lay. She didn't breathe, but I still felt her gaze. I lay my head on the concrete next to hers and I knew she'd always be watching me. I looked into her eyes and time stopped. I was aware of it getting darker and then some time after that dawn coming. They were the happiest hours of my life.'

Gavin stared into the distance, the interview room forgotten.

Teresa waited for several minutes before asking: 'Why didn't you tell anyone?'

Gavin looked at her for a long time. Then, 'She'd come

to me,' he said. 'No one was going to take her away. She was there watching me, with me – she was mine.

'I never saw what happened as an accident. She fell for a reason. I led her there for a reason. Even when the bulldozers came and filled in the lower levels I felt her with me always. It was only after this happened that people started flocking to Green Oaks in their thousands. The expansion went on and the sales shot up. The analysts thought it was all part of the spending boom, but I started to see it differently.

'Do you know in Germany in the Middle Ages, when they tried to build the church in Vilmnitz, the builders couldn't finish the job? Whatever they put up in the daytime fell down at night. So they took a child, gave it a bread-roll in one hand, a light in the other, and set it in a cavity in the foundation, which they mortared shut. The building stood firm after that. Also at Vestenburg Castle – a special seat in the wall for the child. She cried so much that they gave her an apple as they sealed her in. There are entombed children all over Europe bringing prosperity, security, happiness.

'This place chose me. I knew it when I started working here: I felt a special sense of purpose, a mission. I'd walk along the corridors and it felt as if the place was built for me. Everything was the right size, everything felt right to the touch. The walls seemed to hear me, the mirrors talk to me. I heard all the whispers, I knew all the secrets. It chose me and it chose her.'

41

TOP SECRET. DETECTIVE NOTEBOOK.
PROPERTY OF AGENT KATE MEANEY.

Wednesday December 5th VERY IMPORTANT DAY
Stayed at Green Oaks later this evening due to late-night opening.

Suspect in usual location between 4 and 5 p.m. After he left I walked around the malls looking for any other signs of suspicious activity – saw man in electric wheelchair destroy a promotional display of energy drinks – apparently an accident. At 7 p.m. spotted suspect emerging from mirrored door at side of Burger King – disguised as a security guard! Mickey was speechless.

Thursday December 6th
No sign of suspect this evening – worrying? Still can't believe the disguise – exactly as the book had predicted. I am very close to crime now. Mickey is my only confidant. Dad would be proud of us.

Friday December 7th
Got to centre as soon as poss. after Redspoon exam. At 2 p.m. saw suspect patrolling on level 4 in security guard disguise. We followed discreetly, hanging back as much as possible. When will he approach bank?

3 p.m. – Have just witnessed suspect disappear back through mirrored doors by the banks. I think I have to

follow him – he may try and break in from back. Thought he saw my reflection as he passed through door, but he didn't turn around. Detectives have to be brave. Mickey is with me and will be my lookout. I'm going in.

42

If I close my eyes, I'm still in the station. Interviews, paperwork, dark cups of tea in buzzing fluorescent strip-lit rooms. Pressing 'stop', pressing 'record', listening to the tape whirr backwards on the spool, trying to anticipate its juddering halt.

I saw the security guard leaving hand in hand with Lisa Palmer. I thought of calling after him to thank him for his statement, but I don't think he'd have turned back.

I need to get away too, there's nothing to keep me here now. I've been tired for a long time. I want to go somewhere far north where the night never comes and the cold makes you feel new.

Slow traffic but I don't mind. I've got a signed confession. I've got your notebook. I've got your loyal partner sealed in an evidence bag. I'm driving home straight into the setting sun. Along the M5 its low beams push through my tinted windscreen. The light is all around me.

Photo: John McQueen

Catherine O'Flynn was born in Birmingham in 1970, where she grew up in and around her parents' sweet shop as the youngest child of a large family. She has been a teacher, web editor, mystery customer and postwoman. Her first novel draws on her experience of working in record stores – and of growing up as a child intrigued by clues, suspects and methods of detection.

ACKNOWLEDGEMENTS

Thanks to Peter Fletcher, Luke Brown, Lucy Luck, Emma Hargrave, Carl the security guard, plenty of friends and my family.